I'd Rather Kiss You Goodnight

by

Christine Columbus

Surf, Sand and Romance

I'd Rather Kiss You Goodnight

Cover Art by *Tina Lynn Stout*

The Wild Rose Press, Inc.
PO Box 708
Adams Basin, NY 14410-0708
Visit us at www.thewildrosepress.com

Publishing History
First Edition, 2025
Trade Paperback ISBN 978-1-5092-6296-0
Digital ISBN 978-1-5092-6297-7

Surf, Sand and Romance
Published in the United States of America

Dedication

To my family and friends, I thank you for your support, encouragement, and patience in rereading the story. I always appreciate your suggestions and feedback.

To my readers ...Wow! You're the best. I love getting pictures of where you've read the book and for taking the time to post reviews and visit me on social media.

To Sally, who has been asking if I've written another book. Yes, I did, and I hope you enjoy: I'd Rather Kiss You Goodnight.

To Sawmill Book Club, I had so much fun and enjoyed the lively discussion on Chance Meeting.

Praise Comments

"I'D RATHER KISS YOU GOODNIGHT: A fun romcom with twists and turns, a perfect book to read beside the pool."

~Lisa

~*~

"CHANCE MEETING Every plot thread was wrapped up beautifully, leaving me fully satisfied and smiling. I couldn't have asked for a better conclusion. I highly recommend taking a chance on *Chance Meeting*—it's a sweet, emotionally rich romance that's well worth the read."

~Mistflower, Long and Short Reviews

~*~

"CHANCE MEETING is a fast-paced rom-com with loads of comedic relief as Mel and Clay are drawn to each other…There is closure and a happily ever after, and I would love to see this be the start of a series or at least a connected story. Opal and Paula definitely need their own stories to be told."

~Novels Alive by JoAnne

~*~

"I enjoyed I'D RATHER KISS YOU GOODNIGHT, my new favorite book. I love closed door romance. I think your book would make a great movie."

~Patty F

~*~

"I'D RATHER KISS YOU GOODNIGHT is a wonderful romance novel whose main character is able to discover what she wants in life without regrets. Throughout the book she learns to move forward through past disappointments. A very entertaining novel."

~Patty C

Chapter One

After work on Friday, I slipped into a black knit dress with a waterfall front, added a rope of pearls, and embarked on a three-hour drive from Minneapolis to River City, Wisconsin.

Tired and needing a bathroom, I turned into The Club parking lot. With barely enough room, I sped between an oversized black sedan with a sagging bumper and a minivan parked with an oversized Elvis silhouette across the back windshield before finding a space to park two blocks away.

Bernie must have been a local celebrity. I knew little about the man Mom had lived with other than he was president of a non-profit club that provided scholarships for people who wanted to be nurses, and he passed away from cancer a week ago.

Outside the entrance to The Club, I rang the bell, smiled at the camera, and checked my reflection in the window. I looked like a million other women in their forties with blonde highlights in their medium-brown bobbed haircut.

The door buzzed open. I rushed inside, lingering in the doorway as I waited for my eyes to adjust to the dim light. Everyone in The Club swiveled in their chairs and looked before dismissing me as no one of importance. Once again, I was the new kid.

Thirty feet before me, four elderly men stood

beneath a posterboard with Bernie's name and pointed to photos on the poster boards tacked to the beige-painted wall. Their laughter momentarily eclipsed the band but not the buzz of the door.

A rush of warm air sent a shiver up my spine, and goose bumps marching down my arm. And like all the other patrons, I also turned. A sudden tightness in my throat made it difficult to breathe. *Bernie?*

He stepped into the light.

This man was too young to be Bernie. I exhaled.

He flashed a smile that lifted his cheeks and added a few crinkles to both eyes.

If I hadn't needed the restroom, I might have stayed, held out my hand, and introduced myself. Instead of lingering or acknowledging him with a nod, I rushed into the chaos that mirrored the outside parking lot. Chairs and patrons were scattered in complete disorder, with barely enough room to get through. I pushed open the ladies' room door, and the smell and the sounds from the first stall door made me question my needs. Without taking another breath, I moved to the last stall and quickly emptied my bladder.

The last time I had smelled anything so foul was two years ago, when I passed by JR, on my way to the witness stand. The thought of testifying against my ex-fiancé JR still sent shivers down my spine. His gaze bore into me as he sat smugly at the defendant's table.

On the far side of the horseshoe bar, I spotted a few vacant seats. I skirted the edge of the empty dance floor, shimmied behind occupied chairs, and snaked past the windowsills with plants in various stages of decay. Some pots held clumps of crisp brown leaves, and others had limp yellowed vines, but they all looked like they came to The Club to die.

I slid onto the faded red bar stool.

A bartender with bleach blonde hair and penciled-in eyebrows placed two blue plastic chips on the bar.

She had enough makeup to subtract at least ten years, making her somewhere between sixty and seventy.

"The first two drinks are on Bernie." The bartender made the sign of the cross. "Bless his soul. Do you know what you'd like?"

"What would Bernie have?"

"Bourbon Old Fashioned coming up." She scooped up a chip.

As I pulled a ten from my purse, she returned with the drink, and I thanked her.

"Enjoy." She waved the bill before stuffing it into a repurposed pickle jar.

A lowball glass with amber liquid, a slice of orange, and a cherry looked like the answer to a long, difficult week. The first sip sent a shudder down my spine, then a slightly sweet taste, followed by a hint of spice.

The bartender swung past, dropped a red-and-white checkered bowl of popcorn, and asked how I liked my drink.

While nodding, I watched her rush to wait on a woman at the far end of the bar. The salty popcorn and the sweet drink made the perfect combination. With only a few sips left of my drink, I found Mom in a crush of people, everyone was talking at once, and after exchanging a brief hug and letting her know I'd be here for the weekend. I slipped back to my seat and found the waitress had brought me another drink.

The sound of a deep male voice shifted my attention to the left. A smile split my lips. This was the same man who walked in behind me. His eyes were the color of a sea before the storm. Never having seen an ocean, I couldn't swear this was true, but sometimes, you didn't have to see something to know it. This was one of those times. This man stirred a mix of emotions in me…a cocktail of curiosity, attraction, and a hint of apprehension.

"Is this seat taken?"

I stared, no longer remembering what the question was.

He pointed a finger at the chair. His shoulders strained against the fabric of the cotton dress shirt.

Warmth spread across my cheeks as I remembered the question. "No, it's not taken." His eyes and smile drew me closer.

The bartender rushed over, sliding chips before him. "What can I get you?"

He tilted his chin to the left. "What is she drinking?"

My stool swiveled toward him. Our knees bumped. But instead of mumbling an apology. I maintained eye contact. "The bartender can't tell you. It's like doctor-patient confidentiality. Although if you ask me real nice, then I'll tell you." I flashed a toothy smile. *Why am I flirting?* The sight of my half-empty glass supplied the answer. Bourbon. Instead of shying away or summoning the anger and frustration from two years ago, I sat with a poker face.

The bartender smirked.

He held out a hand. "Ty."

"Sal." He had a firm but gentle handshake.

"Short for Sally?"

A simple question. Yet I hesitated, wishing I could think of something clever and knowing I should leave.

"Is this also confidential information?" The right corner of his mouth twitched. He released my hand and slid both chips across the wooden bar. "Give me what she's having. And give her another?"

I motioned for him to come closer. "If you're trying to get me tipsy, it's too late. This is my second, and I don't normally drink anything other than an occasional beer."

"Why tonight? Were you close to Bernie?"

"Yes and no." I tried to clamp my jaw shut, but the words kept coming. "Bernie was my mom's significant other for ten years. Long story. I didn't put any effort into getting to know him, and now, it's too late." I picked up my glass. The ice cubes clinked, and the faint fragrance of fruit and whiskey rose from the short tumbler.

The bartender appeared with two drinks and another bowl of popcorn.

After nodding my thanks I caught the wink she flashed at Ty. Well, who wouldn't? The guy was hot and handsome.

"So—" He turned and held my gaze.

I sensed a connection but feared the attraction had more to do with liquor, the social lubricant, than any actual feelings. The last thing I wanted was to be played for a fool, so I searched for a safe subject and drew a blank. Every day, I had dozens of impersonal conversations, and now, I couldn't think of one generic thing to say.

The tip of his tongue swiped across his bottom lip.

A jolt of desire shot through me. I crossed my legs to counter the sudden pleasure and tried to remember all the hurt and pain from my relationship with JR. Recanting why I was happier without a man did little to squelch my interest. The man beside me with the kind blue eyes and gentle voice lulled me into believing not all men were jackals waiting to devour a woman's heart and drag her into a den of financial ruin. "Are you from River City?"

He brushed a thumb across the faint shadow of whiskers on his chin. "I lived here a long time ago. I'm just back for a few weeks. How about you?"

I glanced at my drink and poked the cherry and orange with my stir stick, watching them sink beneath the surface before floating back. "Just for the weekend to help my mom. Then back to Minneapolis, where I was born and raised."

"Do you like the cities?"

"Everything except winter, construction, and mosquitoes." Did he have a girlfriend? "Where have you been living since you left River City?"

His chest rose and fell as he scanned the room.

Was he looking for someone? I, too, glanced around at what looked like a senior living complex where everyone was waiting for bingo to start. Did he sit down because this was the only vacant chair, or I was the only one under fifty? Hell, with the dark lighting, he might have even mistaken me for forty. Across the room, back by the buffet tables, rose a light laugh. Pleasant, like wind chimes with the musical tone of church bells. A blonde woman stood amongst a crowd with her head tilted back and again produced the sound. She wore a simple black dress, like mine, except hers was fire-engine red and hugged her curves.

Certain he'd be making an excuse to join the lady dressed in red, I picked up the tiny drink spear, jabbed the floating cherry until it resembled a pincushion, and watched it settle to the bottom of the glass.

"My career..."

I craned my neck in his direction.

"Every few years I relocated."

Ignoring the mutilated fruit, I mulled over the possibilities. "Sales?"

"Military retired."

"How old are you? I thought I aged well. But you don't look forty." If her laugh was like a wind chime, then his was the sound of a horn honking, unexpected and gaining my attention.

"Forty-three. I served for twenty-two years. So, how old are you?"

"I'd say guess, but we both know if you guess thirty, then I'd know you were trying to pick me up at a funeral." I scowled. "And if you guess fifty, I'd feel depressed, not that I'm that far off at forty-seven."

His eyebrow arched as he gave a slight nod. "You look amazing." The wind chime grew louder and drew his attention, and the moment his gaze locked onto the red dress, he furrowed his brows and grimaced.

I've never seen a man's face during a colonoscopy, but I'm sure the pinched facial features were the same. Wanting to ease his discomfort, I brushed a finger across his forearm. "Were you ever deployed?"

He nodded.

"What was it like?"

"Tonight's about celebrations." He smiled. "I don't want to dwell in the past."

"Me, either." I raised my glass.

He tapped his rim on my Old Fashioned. "To future endeavors."

Was he hiding something worse than me? And endeavors? We'd likely never see each other again. As I struggled to put it all together...I noticed him staring. "What?"

"Will you do me a favor?"

I tensed. *Fifteen minutes into the conversation and he's going to ask for money, a ride home, or sex.* The last item on the list made me smile.

"Let's be the first couple on the dance floor." He again moistened his bottom lip with a quick lick.

I glanced at the band. A bald man with a tuft of white played the keyboard as the lead singer strummed a guitar and sang, but the drummer had short, spikey, silver-gray hair with red and purple highlights. She looked like she was having the time of her life. Did she ever feel frustrated being a musician? All that practice and commitment and then you're playing, and you have no idea if anyone's listening, like when I went out to dinner with co-workers, and everyone was on their phones.

"Come on." He nudged me. "I think Bernie would want us to. One dance to celebrate life."

"Why not?" I exhaled, knowing great stories and poor decisions started the same way. I picked up my glass.

"You don't need anymore." He placed his right hand on my wrist.

Nodding, I left the drink and followed him onto the space before the band.

Ty's right hand slid to my hip as his left hand laced

through my fingers.

The music started.

Suddenly, standing in the center of the empty floor, reminded me of exiting the witness stand, and instead of following his lead, I stumbled.

His grip tightened. "Relax. No one is watching us." He kept moving clockwise.

I glanced around. Everyone seemed occupied with their companions. This wasn't anything like the trial. I could feel the tension drain from my shoulders. We passed the *Celebrate Live* poster, and before I could get a look, I spun in the opposite direction. "I saw the photo of Mom and Bernie dancing during Oktoberfest weekend."

He gave a reassuring squeeze. "I think there's a song about if you get the chance to dance. So many no longer can." He moved across the floor effortlessly.

"Yes, a Lee Ann Womack song "I Hope You Dance." Wendy, my supervisor, would play this all the time at work. She passed in February." I faltered. "You're not dying, are you?"

His laughter rang out. "I hope not. No, I'm trying to enjoy simple pleasures."

I closed my eyes and inhaled. His scent was reminiscent of the crisp smell of cool autumn days, apple orchards, and flannel shirts.

"Ever listen to the song "Live Like You Were Dying"?" His grasp tightened, and he switched direction.

"Tim McGraw. But I have no desire to go skydiving."

"But you came out on the dance floor."

The encouragement in his voice made me wonder

if I could let go of JR and the past. Or did the desire to live in the moment have more to do with the passing of Wendy and Bernie? A slight pressure on my shoulder stilled my thoughts.

His right arm rose as his left slid down my spine and propelled me forward.

After a graceful turn, I was back in his arms.

"Where did you go to?"

I squashed the desire to pull him closer. "Just thinking."

"About?"

"Do you believe in signs?"

His smile faded into neutrality before a grin broke out, wrinkling the corners of both eyes. "Stop signs or divine intervention?"

"Spiritual, I guess. Wendy believed in psychics and messages from the dead. After she passed, I started finding heart-shaped objects in the oddest places." Did Wendy send Ty? Should I pinch him to see if he's real?

He raised his right eyebrow. "So, do you think Bernie will send you anything?"

"I hadn't thought about it." As the song's last notes faded, I remained in his embrace, hoping the band would play another slow song. I didn't think this guy was my prince, but for tonight, I saw no harm in pretending. I never thought the hurt and betrayal would fade, but swaying in Ty's arms felt like drinking a spiced pumpkin latte while wearing a flannel shirt. *Perfect.*

No longer the only couple on the dance floor, I glanced at the other couples poised and waiting when a glimmer on the floor caught my attention. I squinted and pointed. "Did someone drop an earring?"

Ty slid a hand lower as he bent and scooped the object from the floor. "Looks like you have your answer. Dimes from Bernie and hearts from Wendy."

The band shifted to a seventies tune "Three Times a Lady" by the Commodores.

After a spin, he slowed the tempo and the distance between us disappeared. "To hold you…"

I slipped my hand to his mid-back and felt his muscles ripple. I closed my eyes. *To feel you…*

He leaned slightly to the right.

Instinctively, I responded to the subtle shifts, moving around the floor like I had danced with him a hundred times before. The song's last notes vibrated, and I stood plastered against him with no intention of stepping away until hearing the first notes of the Macarena. Cool air replaced the heat of his body.

At the edge of the dance floor, he slowly released my hand. "Thank you."

With a racing heart over the shared moment, I retraced my steps to the bar stool. Twisting my pearls, I thought of Cinderella. *When the clock strikes closing time will I be without a prince?* After all I'd been through, I still want a happily ever after ending, riding into the sunset with a man by my side. I slid onto the barstool and felt the weight of his palm brush across my left shoulder.

He sat, holding up the silver coin. "Mind if I keep it?"

"Not at all. I've three heart-shaped rocks I found on my kitchen table at home—" Heat rushed to my cheeks. What if Wendy started sending men? The image of Ty sitting on my table did strange things to my insides.

"It's getting louder in here. Did you just ask if you should take me home?"

I mouthed a perfect *no* and added a head shake for emphasis. God, I hoped I hadn't said that aloud.

His facial muscles twitched.

What a tease? I swatted his forearm.

With a tilt of his head, he motioned to come closer.

I leaned in, wondering if it was alcohol or if this was the start of something?

"Let's get out of here."

His words caressed my ear. I nodded. Sitting this close to Ty created feelings I didn't want to explore. If his lips brushed mine, would I remember the pain and embarrassment from the past? Or would his kiss keep me planted in the moment? I fanned my face. Hopefully, the crisp night air would clear my head. Three drinks were two too many.

He reached for my right hand.

I hesitated. Just for tonight, I'd live in the moment. Come Sunday, I'd be back in Minneapolis with nothing but a memory of Ty. I slid my fingers across his palm and followed him, zigzagging to the back door.

Outside, the night air cooled my flushed skin. I relaxed my grip. To my surprise, his clasp tightened, and warmth radiated.

"I'm kind of hungry. Do you know if Chili Dawg off Main or Pickle-Dilly Sandwiches are still open?" He swung our arms.

The gesture made me smile. "No, but food sounds good."

"Let's try Bob's Buzzard."

Three blocks later, I spotted the flashing neon buzzard and entered the historic red brick building. The lights were subdued, and the smell of deep-fried food and grilled meats had my mouth watering.

To the right, a few patrons sat on bar stools, staring at TVs or the assortment of bottles displayed on the glass shelves. To the left were booths with emerald-green upholstered seats and worn wooden tables. I followed the waitstaff to a corner booth in the back.

"This looks great." Ty nudged me. "Sit."

I slipped between the table and the padded bench seat.

Ty slid in beside me.

What's he doing? Maybe he doesn't like people watching him eat.

He smashed closer. "I prefer not to sit with my back to the wall. Besides, it's kind of cozy."

After ordering, I relaxed against the back of the booth.

"Tell me about Wendy."

Dozens of memories flashed back as I smiled. "We met at a fund-raising event. Wendy was an animal shelter volunteer dressed up as a wiener dog, and I was the sponsor. Well, not me, but JR's construction firm. Instant friendship." I smiled and shook my head. "After the event, I went with Wendy for drinks, and she didn't bother changing out of her costume. It was quite the night."

I told him about sewing and donating quilts to the animal shelter and how I had lost lots of friends over the closing of the construction firms. Without Wendy, I became a homebody. The whole time we talked, I resisted the urge to pinch myself. He seemed too good to be true. Now, more than ever, I wanted to text Wendy and tell her about him. Was Ty missing anyone?

The sound of footsteps and mouthwatering aromas stalled further questions.

With a steady hand the server set sizzling deep-fried gator fingers and armadillo eggs with a side of ranch dressing and honey mustard on the table.

Deep-fried, bacon-wrapped chicken tenders—stuffed with pepper jack cheese and jalapenos—were almost the size of baseballs. The gator fries looked like deep-fried shrimp or fat calamari.

Forty-five minutes later, I exited the bar with a full belly. With his hand in mine, I window-shopped as our path took us past a bookstore, coffee shops, and an antique store. Not wanting the evening to end, I hesitantly stepped into the parking lot at The Club. I noticed him fidgeting, and instead of eye contact, he gazed at the pavement. "What?"

He shrugged.

"You look like you want to say something."

"Yeah, I should have mentioned—"

I stepped back. Tension stiffened every muscle in my body. "You're married. Or you have a girlfriend or boyfriend?" I ground my molars together. *Men, they're all the same.*

"What?" He reached forward, palms opened wide. "There's no one."

Scrutinizing his face for obvious signs of lying...no raised eyebrows, blushing or stammering. Was he telling the truth?

"I promise." He tipped my chin slightly before lowering his mouth.

The first tentative touch was like a welcomed summer breeze, gentle and caressing. I leaned closer, the kiss deepened, and then—passion, heat, and flames enveloped us.

He tangled his fingers in my hair, and the beating of his heart pulsed against my chest, causing everything to fade except the taste of his mouth, the feel of his body, and a sense of urgency. Why had I waited almost two years? I shivered, wanting more.

A light flashed from The Club, and the sound of my name echoed in the darkness along with the unmistakable sound of the wind chime laugh.

I heard his quick intake of air.

The embrace turned clumsy. Instead of being held by a man, I felt like I was embracing a mannequin.

"Sally!" The word echoed again off the building wall.

I stepped back and turned toward the building.

Mom stomped closer.

The blonde-haired woman in the red dress waved her arms.

Ty brushed a finger against my forearm, turned, and walked away.

I swallowed the word, *wait*, as the cool night air rushed in to replace the heat from his body. Should I chase after him?

Bony fingers clutched my biceps.

I gasped and spun around, half expecting to see the ghost of Wendy or Bernie, but instead, I looked into Mom's green eyes.

"Come on, Sal."

Swallowing, I gave a quick backward glance. *Ty, please turn around.*

Chapter Two

Two hours later, I stepped into the spare bedroom, puzzled over Mom's comments on the ride home. Half a dozen times she had mentioned not wanting to move. Was her mind beginning to slip? I swept my gaze over the three twin beds with matching bedspreads and the faded blue-and-white striped wallpaper in the bedroom that had once belonged to Bernie's sons. The only thing left from their childhood was damage done to a plaster wall from what I heard was one of their many fights. I dropped my overnight backpack on the middle bed and shifted my thoughts to Ty.

Naked, I slid into the cool, crisp cotton sheets, enveloped in the scent of fabric softener. Curled on my side, I felt my thighs cling to each other like plastic wrap and flopped onto my back. I wasn't sure I wanted another relationship, but something about Ty made me wish I'd exchanged numbers. At least now, I didn't have to wonder if he'd call or come up with some clever text or meme to let him know I was thinking about him. I snuggled deeper into the bed, replaying our conversations, recalling the slight curve of his lips, the darkening of his eyes, and the kiss. He was like a favorite song. I could listen to him all night long.

In the morning I awoke disorientated in a bed way too small, leaped from the bed, gathered my things, and rushed to the only bathroom.

Under the hot stream of water, I felt the tension ebb from my shoulders. If the house had more than one bathroom, I would have lingered. After quickly styling my hair and adding makeup, I glanced at the mirror attached to the door. *Not bad.* I emerged feeling refreshed and ready to tackle Mom.

In the kitchen, a slight summer breeze filtered through the window, and sunshine twinkled across the dirty dishes in the sink. Leaning against the chipped plastic melon-orange counter, I scrolled through social media.

"Put your phone down," Mom scolded.

"You're up early." I stuffed the phone into my pocket.

Mom's gray hair was now blaze-orange, her black tank top showed off cleavage that would never sag, and her jeans hung low on her waist. The only thing old about my mother was her name, Mabel.

At the sound of the front door opening, I cocked my head and listened to the approaching footsteps.

A man stepped from the shadows of the hallway and into the kitchen.

I widened my gaze and gasped for air. *No way.*

"Um, morning, Sal." Ty cleared his throat and ran an index finger under the white shirt collar.

Anger knotted my stomach. I sucked in the last bit of oxygen in the room. *Bernie's son, Ty.* I balled my fingers into rock-hard fists.

Mom sprang from her seat. The wooden kitchen chair teetered and crashed to the floor. She rushed toward Ty, made a fist, and cocked back her elbow.

"Don't hit him." I hustled forward, pushing her toward the front door. The last thing I needed this weekend was to bail her out of jail for assault charges.

As her footsteps echoed down the hall, the burning sensation in my stomach turned sour. "Ty. Bernie's son."

Instead of denial, he gave a slight nod and reached forward.

Jumping backward, I watched with satisfaction as his hands clasped nothing but air.

"Sal, I need to talk to you about last night? I wanted to tell you."

Fearing my voice would break, I swallowed the angry retort and strode down the hall without answering. He had so many chances to tell me and said nothing. How could he lie? Men, they're all the same. Why do I always fall for their sweet words? I pushed the wooden front door open.

"Sally! Don't let the door slam."

Grasping the warped frame, I hesitated, then let go, and waited for the thunderous crash.

Thud.

Mom stood beside my red SUV, shaking her head and rolling her eyes like a slot machine. "Pathetic."

I stood outside the vehicle and stared at my empty hands. So much for a grand exit. "I'll be back. I need my keys." Storming back inside, I bypassed Ty with a defiant stride. "You can wipe that smile off your face." In the spare bedroom, I grabbed my purse and met him in the hallway.

"You don't have to go."

"There is no reason for me to stay." Smirking, I brushed past him, climbed inside the car, and waited for Mom to buckle the seat belt. The dash clock flashed ten. Too late for breakfast and too early for lunch.

"Want to get ice cream?"

Mom stared at the front windshield, rumbling in the seat like a teakettle, ready to let off some steam.

"Ice cream, it is."

She rolled down her window. "Take a left on Third to get to Pearl. It's faster."

I continued down Main Street.

"Sally, it's okay to take a different route."

At our fourth red light, I glanced over.

"You should have taken Third."

"And miss all this quality time I'm spending with you."

"Hmph." She crossed her arms.

"Sorry." I sighed, knowing this had been a tough week. Bernie had been her longest relationship. Most entanglements lasted a couple of years. If she had married instead of cohabitating, I could have been in the record books for having the most stepdads.

I turned left onto a cobblestone street and found an open meter in River City's historic downtown district. Quaint brick buildings, ornate coin-operated parking meters, and tree-lined sidewalks stood between the mighty Mississippi River and the six-hundred-foot sandstone bluffs. I walked down the street to Sweets.

Like every other tourist town on the Mississippi River, Sweet's boasted fudge, candy, souvenirs, handmade waffle cones, and ice cream. The bells connected to the door jingled as I entered the historic soda shop. I inhaled the sweet aroma of baked waffle cones, vanilla, sugar, and chocolate.

To the right were glass counters and various candies, and to the left stood an old wooden counter with two teenage girls in white dress shirts, black bow ties, and aprons.

I watched them lift stainless steel covers and scoop ice cream into the waffle cones.

With her head barely visible above the wooden counter, Mom stepped forward. "A scoop of Blue Moon in a waffle cone and—"

"And I'll have vanilla."

"You always get the same thing. Try something else."

"Fine, give me the Mississippi Mud." I pulled a few paper napkins from the dispenser.

Mom reached for the neon-blue ice cream looking like an actress accepting an award as she sauntered out the door.

Moments later, I followed with my cone stuffed with chocolate, marshmallows, nuts, and ribbons of chocolate-sandwich-cookie crumbles. Before my first lick, I heard Mom let out a banshee scream. Through the glare of the late morning sun, I saw her rush toward a man.

I stepped away from the commotion and into the shade of the building. Bernie had been dead less than a week. Had she found a new boyfriend? Was this a lover's quarrel? I lowered my head and pretended to be an innocent bystander. From my new position, I spotted Mom, but the lamppost blocked my view of the man's face.

The man stood motionless, like a soldier at attention. He turned.

"Oh, no. Ty."

"Ohhhhh," emanated from the crowd.

I repositioned myself. Mom's blue ice cream was no longer in her waffle cone. I stared at the hand-churned ice cream clinging to Ty's white shirt. Against my will, images from last night flashed before my eyes. I remembered my hand on that same hard chest.

"You're heartless!" Mom screamed as the large scoop of bright-blue slid down his stomach and hit the sidewalk.

The ice cream lay lifeless between their feet.

A young mother used her arms and hands to block the view from her two big-eyed girls, who pointed and giggled.

Two teenage boys jumped from their skateboards. The wheels clacked against the red brick.

I half expected one of them to shout, *Fight, fight, fight,* as they clambered onto the curb.

Mom stood with pursed lips and arms crossed.

Having received that look many times, I stepped back, leaned against the cool limestone bricks, and greedily licked my ice cream. *Would she come for more ammunition?*

"Mabel, let's be reasonable." Ty held both hands with palms up and stepped back.

"Mrs. Ridel to you. And don't you go anywhere until you clean up that mess." She wiggled her bent finger toward a decorative black iron trash can.

By this time, a few more people had gathered.

I stood on tippy-toes to see if he'd picked up her ice cream.

Ty's forehead and nose scrunched as he scanned the gathering crowd.

The anger and humiliation I felt toward him dissipated. I swallowed, hoping I wouldn't regret this decision, and pushed past the mother with the two girls and grabbed Mom's elbow. "Let's go," I said in what I hoped sounded like a stern voice. Never having had children, I had no idea how to render people helpless without raising my voice.

With a downcast gaze, she muttered and fell into step.

Suddenly, I no longer felt like a child. *Did our roles reverse?* After walking past the six-foot pelican statues, I directed her to a bench facing the Mississippi River. "Do you want to tell me what that was all about?"

"Ty wants me to move out of my house." She sat straighter and gestured with her hands. "I told him he had to be joking. In twenty-five years, he's never been home. Yet, he gets a fourth of the house. It isn't right. It isn't fair."

"Why would Ty want to kick you out of the house? Did Bernie have a will?"

Mom nodded. "Yes, we all went to the lawyers on Thursday. Remember, I told you. Bernie left the house for the three boys and me. He left his motorcycle for you."

"Yeah, yeah." I nodded and made the appropriate sounds. "It was nice he thought of me, but you can have the bike."

"The will states you can't sell it unless you can drive it. You have six months."

"What? Why? This makes no sense. Why give me something when he knew—"

"Who cares about the cycle? What am I going to do?"

I stood, stepped over to the trash, and tossed the remainder of my cone into the garbage. "Rent an apartment or buy the sons' shares out. I'm taking a quick lap around the park. I need to think."

She stood and shadowed my steps to the river's edge.

A white tugboat with red trim pushed twelve loaded metal barges past us.

She needed a place to live. Where? An apartment? Senior community? Or with me? At the thought, I couldn't stop an intense shiver that rocked my body. Living together was not an option.

Mom grasped my forearm. "Sally. Are you even listening?"

I nodded and loosened her talon grip.

"If I stayed in the house, I could get roommates. We'd share the expenses. Can you talk to Ty? I could write up papers, and when I'm dead, they could sell. At seventy it shouldn't be too much longer."

"What?" I skidded to a halt and glanced from the top of her spikey hair to her running shoes. "You're in fine health, you act like women half your age, and you will live at least another twenty years. I doubt they'll want to wait years before selling the house. But I'll talk to one of the other brothers."

"No." She shook her head. "You need to talk to Ty. The other two will go along with whatever he wants."

"That makes no sense. Isn't Travis the oldest?"

Mom shrugged and walked past the stone water fountain with kids splashing.

Fishing boats, pontoons, speedboats, and tugboats jammed the river on weekends, making it look like a rush hour commute on a holiday weekend.

Today, I ignored the traffic idling past River Park. Where would Mom live? I had no idea if I needed to look for income-based housing or a modest apartment.

"Sally, where do you keep drifting off to? Is there something going on with you and Ty? Amber said you were dancing at The Club last night. And in the parking lot, the way you two were groping and kissing, looked like you were auditioning for a B-rated movie. He's a looker but also trying to toss me to the curb. I'm not against you having fun. God knows you could use a little pleasure…just not with him."

Heat shot from the pit of my stomach to my cheeks. When I kissed Ty, I had no idea he was one of Bernie's sons. I clenched my hands. What else wasn't he telling me? I should have jabbed him with my ice cream cone.

Chapter Three

After the Saturday mid-morning walk, I drove back to the house with my ice cream sitting like a lump between my stomach and mouth. How could I convince Bernie's sons to let Mom stay in the house? The solution to the problems struck me. If I found her an apartment, I wouldn't need to confront the brothers or have her move to Minneapolis. "Mom, let's go look at places to live."

"Sal, I'm tired. It's been a long week. I need to lie down."

I glanced over and noticed the dark circles under her eyes and the pallor in her face. "Sure. Okay." I turned the corner and saw no vehicles parked in front of the house. "Looks like Ty's left. Guess I'll have to chat with them later."

"They'll be back." Mom stepped through the front door, paused, and clutched my forearm. "Remember, I need to be at The Club by five thirty. You're helping with the Chicken Q."

"I should go home. You don't need company. I could look at apartments online and set up appointments. What's your budget?"

Mom dug her fingers deeper. "You need to convince the boys to let me stay. Besides, without Bernie to help, we'll need extra people at the event."

"Fine." I pried her hand loose and watched her

walk away. After a couple of laps around the living room, I wandered into the kitchen and over to the sink. Humming a tune from last night, I washed the stack of dishes. After setting the last scrubbed pan into the drying rack, I wiped the crumbs from the table.

The front door creaked. Footsteps echoed down the hallway, stopping behind me. "Sal."

I spun around with a furrowed brow. "What do you want?"

Ty sighed and held up his hands. "Is this a good time to talk?"

"No." I squeezed the dingy rag in my hand until water dripped onto the floor. "The time to talk would have been last night."

He raked his fingers through short, dark hair. "I wanted to say something, but—"

"The point is…" I straightened to my five feet seven inches, slinging words like arrows aimed at his lying heart. "You didn't say a word."

He stepped closer.

I retreated.

He advanced.

When I bumped into the wall, I realized our faces were inches apart. I sniffed. Instead of an apple orchard, he smelled like cotton candy. Was he still wearing the same shirt Mom had decorated with her scoop of Blue Moon? I placed both hands on his chest and tried to shove him. "Ew. Get away from me."

"You sound like a sibling." He twisted his mouth and made the sound of someone gagging. "Travis told me to stay away. I should have listened, but I kissed you. Ew."

Using the counter for leverage, I pushed him back

a few feet. "Where was your righteous judgment last night when we kissed? I heard you murmur my name as you pulled me close. Your behavior was anything but brotherly."

He widened his gaze. "Oh, Sal. I think you were the one moaning."

"Whatever? Just like you're not the guy kicking an old lady to the curb. She's lived in the house for ten years." I stomped past him and tossed the rag into the sink.

The front door slammed.

A moment later, Travis entered the kitchen.

Trevor, the youngest brother, followed on his heels.

The three brothers looked nothing alike. Ty was the only one with blue eyes and clean shaven. Travis had dark brown eyes, a head of red curls, a moustache, and was over six feet. The youngest Trevor also had brown eyes but was chunky, about my height, bald, with a bushy black beard and a quick smile.

"Hey, Sally." Travis stopped abruptly, pushing the red curls from his eyes. "What's going on?"

Ty shook his head. "Nothing."

Trevor rushed over and wrapped his arms around me. "Hey, sorry I didn't get to chat with you last night." He rocked us back and forth.

I held him tight, patting his back. *Sweet Trevor.*

Someone cleared their throat, loudly.

Trevor backed away from my embrace.

Travis stepped forward with an awkward side shoulder hug. "There were so many people last night. Yeah and sorry. Dad told us about your troubles. Real shame. I liked JR. Everyone did."

Flashing a weak smile, I rolled my eyes. "Well, now JR has a chance to make new friends in prison."

Travis stepped closer to Ty, giving him a friendly punch in the arm. "Trevor and I stopped by to see an agent about listing the house."

Trevor nodded vigorously.

"What?" I advanced, looking past the curls and made eye contact.

Travis held up his hands. "Hey, Sal, it's okay. Your mom knows her—"

"Doesn't Mom get a say in this?" I widened my stance. "Can you legally kick her out? Doesn't she have squatter rights or something?"

Ty moved in closer.

The three of us formed a triangle.

I shifted my glare from Travis to Ty.

"If you want to encourage your mom to hire a lawyer, go ahead." Ty maintained eye contact. "The attorney already explained the options. They weren't married, and her name wasn't on the title. The next installment of property taxes is due at the end of August, and I want out of this town."

I exhaled, turned, and lightly brushed the fingers of my right hand across Trevor's sleeve. "Would it hurt if she stayed a few more years? I can help with the taxes. She could get roommates."

Trevor lifted his bald head, glanced at Ty and Travis, and shrugged. "Makes no difference to me."

Travis and his mop of curls encroached on my space.

"Ty's leaving, and Trevor can't swing a hammer, so that would leave me running over to fix leaky roofs and drippy faucets. I don't have the time."

Ty paced. "Travis is right. I've been here less than two weeks and can see a dozen things that need repairs. The house is a hundred years old. There are holes in the living room wall, cracks in the bedroom ceiling, and tiles falling off the shower in the bathroom. The basement needs waterproofing and the light fixtures—"

"Enough!" I threw my hands in the air. "I get it. The house needs work."

Travis brushed the hair from his eyes. "Amber said if we're selling the house, as-is, the time to list is now."

I wanted to tell Travis to get a haircut or a clip but focused on the issue. "Wait until she has a place to live."

Travis stomped, and the massive curls bounced. "Why can't she live with you?"

"I have a one-bedroom apartment." I almost choked on the words I spewed so easily. *OMG. I'm a liar. Who lives in a two-bedroom, two-bath apartment.* Was I no better than JR and Ty, lying to get what I wanted? I loved Mom but couldn't live with her. The couple of weekends I spent with her each year were enough. The first twenty-four hours were manageable, but then day two came, and she'd start telling me how to live my life. After gritting my teeth and nodding for hours, I'd come undone and grab the backpack from the floor. She'd yell something about me being too sensitive and had been all my life.

Studying the pattern on the chipped floor, I paced. If Mom lived with me, I'd feel trapped. Where would I go to escape?

"Sal."

Ty and his bright-blue eyes stopped my progress.

"Maybe it would be easier if your mom wasn't two

and a half hours away. She's getting older. Could you get a two-bedroom apartment?"

"Mom has lived in River City for ten years." I planted my feet. "Her friends, doctors, and The Club are all here. There would be nothing for her in Minneapolis. She never liked the big city." I cringed at how easily a second lie rolled off my tongue. "If you wait, I'm sure I could find her an apartment by fall. Give me three or four months at the most. Then list the house." I clasped my hands together. Hopefully, between the two of us, we could save enough for the first and last month's rent along with a damage deposit. Once the house sold...

"No wonder my ears were on fire." Mom's orange hair lit up the kitchen. "All of you gabbing about me. I'm not dead like your daddy, and I sure don't need you, Sally, to fight my battles."

"Fine." The word whistled between my pursed lips as I clenched my jaw and started toward the front door.

"Wait," Mom yelled. "Don't be so sensitive. I just got off the phone with Amber. Like one of those déjà vu moments. She mentioned you boys stopped to see her, and after looking into the market, suggested flipping the house instead of listing it. We could get at least one hundred thousand more for a turnkey home."

"Amber!" Ty stomped. "I say list it." He crossed his arms. "But with a different agent."

I glanced from a glaring Ty to his grinning brothers, who looked like they wanted to high five each other. "Amber?"

"Last night, she wore the prettiest red dress." Mom ran her hands over her hips and swayed. "She told me Hank can get a discount on paint and plaster. Fred can help with wiring and Pete with plumbing."

"But…" Ty paced in the opposite direction. "They won't work for free. Did Amber mention what it would cost? Labor is expensive. There goes your profit."

"Well, you're mistaken." Mom stepped in front of Ty. "Bernie had been president of The Club for the past eight years. And last night I spoke to all of them, and they'd help anyway they could help. Sally will come down every weekend. She's strong and will work for free. You still want that motorcycle of your daddy's?"

I shook my head. "Wait. I need to—"

"Want to trade if for my portion of the house?" Ty cocked his head.

"Time-out." I held up my hands. Why didn't Bernie give the bike to his son? Did he see an issue with the house and want me to help Mom? But why make me learn to drive? "I don't care about—"

"Tell you what." Mom paced like a detective in a courtroom, ready to reveal the murderer. "You help flip the house, and it's yours."

"What if Sal doesn't get a motorcycle endorsement?"

I shifted closer to Ty. "When I get a license." Fingers clasped the back of my bicep, I turned.

Mom winked, multiple times before relaxing her grip.

Rubbing my arm, I watched her buzz about the room. Now wasn't the time to argue. I'd hear the plan and then decide. "Hmmm," Mom hummed. "The attorney mentioned after the allotted time the bike would go to The Club. Let me do some checking, but I'm sure the board members would sign the title over for a substantial donation. The bike was appraised at forty thousand. I'd bet they'd take twenty-five, seeing you're his son."

"Deal." He held out a hand. "But Amber isn't the real estate agent."

"No deal. I already told Amber she had the job. Shame to give up the extra twenty-five thousand and the bike. List the house. Come on, Sal."

A slight jab caught me in the ribs. "Just a second."

"Ty, man. Give this Amber thing a rest." Travis stepped closer. "I could use the extra cash. It'll only be a weekend or two."

Mom started for the door. "When you boys figure it out, let me know."

I sighed and trailed after her. Would I end up with a roommate? Why was everyone being so unreasonable? And why didn't Ty like Amber?

****

On the drive to The Club, Mom refused to answer questions and insisted she had everything under control.

"Okay, but I'm not working on the house." I pulled into the parking lot and as I shifted into Park, the door ajar alarm rang.

Mom climbed out of the front seat. "Come on, stop dawdling." She glanced over and sighed. "Just meet me inside."

At the back entrance, I caught up. "You can have the money from the bike."

She didn't respond and continued down the hall with framed photos of the past club presidents, around the bar, and paused by tables.

I heard a familiar voice from the hallway. *Ty?*

Mom pointed to the storage closet. "Sally, put the sign outside."

"Yeah, in a second. I want to know what they decided."

"Now!" Mom clapped. "Hop to it."

I shook my head. "In a minute."

"Please, Sal." She folded her hands in prayer. "I need your help. I can't do this alone."

"Okay." I stepped into the storage closet and flipped on the light. Wooden shelves loaded with toilet paper, containers, cups, plates, and plastic utensils lined the wall to the right. To the left were mops, buckets, brooms, and the three-by-five-foot wooden sandwich board.

"Here, let me help." Ty stepped closer.

"Why are you here?"

"To help with the sign."

"No, at The Club?"

"Your mom told me to." He snorted.

I swallowed my grin. Even though he had on a clean cream-colored T-shirt, I could still imagine the halo of blue forever imprinted over his abdomen. "Are your brothers here, too?"

"No, they volunteered last month and the month before...don't get me started." He hoisted the sign and stepped into the hallway.

I followed him to the front of the building and helped with placing the weathered, hand-painted sign. I glanced over and watched a slight smile curve his lips.

He made eye contact.

Instead of looking away, I met his gaze. "You know, I regret not being the one who stabbed you with a cone."

He slipped his right hand over the erupting smile.

"Excuse me." A woman with three kids pointed.

"What's a Chicken-Q?"

I left Ty to explain they cooked the chicken on the large outside grill and served the meal with the two sides.

****

For two hours, I stayed out of sight in the basement, washing dishes and playing games on my phone. At a little after eight, I heard footsteps and turned. *Ty.*

"I wasn't sure where you had disappeared to." He walked over to the sink. "Looks like you got stuck washing dishes."

Water dripped from both hands. Why was he so damn good-looking, and why did kissing him feel so good?

He grabbed a white apron and wrapped the ties around his waist.

Last night, I knew nothing about him. Now, I knew he was practically my half-brother, and I was contemplating giving up my celibate life. I exhaled as the heat from the pit of my stomach warmed me more than a strenuous workout. I shifted my attention from the ties to his mouth.

He laughed. "So, you like my apron?"

"No." Another lie. "You're evicting my mom." I turned and sprayed the remaining food off the stack of dirty plates. Is this how JR started? A little fib about having a prison record?

"Hey. I'm not some slum lord kicking your mom out." His words tickled my neck.

I spun around. "You agreed Mom can stay."

He shifted and readjusted the tie on his apron. "Um, no. Not exactly."

Sighing, I leaned against the commercial stainless-steel sink.

"There's a family meeting tomorrow."

"About?" I leaned into his personal space.

"It all hinges on if your mom can get The Club to sign over the bike for a donation."

Standing tall, I leaned closer as excitement bubbled. "I'll get the motorcycle license."

"You'd do that for me?"

"No." I shook my head. "Not for you, but because Mom and I could use the money. So, is your issue with Travis' idea or Amber?"

He turned and stepped away.

Satisfaction settled through me as I watched him push full racks of sprayed dinnerware through the sterilizer.

The plates clicked and clacked. Water whooshed.

I wanted to pursue the conversation, but the noise made talking impossible. After spraying the last plate, I stepped back and untied my apron.

As he shucked off his apron, he bumped my left hip. "Any plans for tonight?"

"Yep, giving Mom a ride home." I walked to the stairwell. Music from the band drifted down the stairs. Was this the same band that played last night? I stepped from the hallway and pushed away the memory of dancing with Ty. I crossed the empty dance floor, humming along to "Take a Chance on Me."

With a wave and nod, I acknowledged Mom and her friends before moving to the far side of the horseshoe bar. I sat in the same seat as last night and pulled out my phone. Nine o'clock. In an hour, most people would leave. If the bartender didn't need Mom's help to close, then we'd be out of here by ten thirty.

After ordering a diet cola, I searched through *Adopt a Dog* and *Pet Finders* before switching to social media. A memory of Wendy popped up. A year ago, we were sipping wine and having a pedicure. *Forty-one. What's the point?*

"Hey."

Fumbling like a kid getting caught passing notes in class, I tucked the phone into my pocket and shrugged. "Hey, Ty." A quick dismissive glance turned into a scowl. After serving chicken dinners and washing dishes, I felt grimy and needed a shower. While he looked sexy, like a model in a magazine wearing a T-shirt and denim jeans. I could feel the edge of my lip curl. And he wouldn't even admit he felt something last night. Accusing me of getting all gooey when he did all the pursuing.

He leaned closer.

Gazing into those lying eyes, I knew what I had to do. Grabbing both shoulders, I pulled him close and planted a kiss. Not a sisterly kind of smooch. A passionate, let's-get-out-of-here-and-get-a-room type of kiss. He wrapped an arm around my shoulders, and instead of getting lost in the moment, I waited. Teasing with my tongue, I deepened the kiss, pulling him closer. Need pulsated and curled my toes, and for a brief second, I forgot time and place.

Then he moaned.

Mustering my last bit of strength, I ended the experiment and sat back. "Ha." I wheezed. "You see what you just did? Melt and murmur."

He laughed, but instead of a honking horn, the sound was pure merriment. With shoulders shaking and abs quivering, tears formed in his eyes as the rumble of laughter continued.

I glared at the tear tumbling down his cheek, pushed the bar stool back, and stood.

"Don't go." He rested a hand on my forearm. "You surprise the hell out of me. Please."

Settling against the back of the chair, I crossed my arms. "Now tell me I was right."

"If you're asking if that was the best kiss of my life, yeah. Although last night was good, too."

Best kiss. Suddenly, a grin creased my heated cheeks. With the tension from my shoulders melting, I leaned closer. *Is this sarcasm?* The slight tingle in my lips vanished. "You're full of crap and a liar—"

"First," he lowered his voice. "I never lied. If you had asked, I would have told you Bernie was my dad. I hate dishonest people." He stood and placed his clenched fist on the bar. "Do you believe in signs?"

"Like knocking on wood." I smirked, wondering where this was going.

"Today, I stepped out of the trailer and found this hanging on a branch." He flipped his fist over.

"A dime, a heart-shaped leaf?"

He uncurled his fingers. A small red-white-and-blue quilted heart lay in his palm.

The stitching looked perfect. I flipped the scraps of material over. *I Need a Home* was stitched in black.

"Last night, you told me you had hearts on your table. Now I have a heart that needs a home." He folded my fingers over the tiny quilting.

I uncurled my hand. The little heart was exquisite. I could stitch something similar with Wendy's, Bernie's, and my dad's names.

"Hello, I'm Ty."

His blue eyes shone like a perfect summer sky.

"Bernie's son, and you must be Sally. I noticed your smile across the room, and something told me you were a great kisser."

Heat rushed to my cheeks. "We've met. You're the guy whose eyes matched the ice cream stain on his shirt."

He laughed.

The tension vanished like early morning fog from the river.

"Do you want to get some fresh air and form an alliance against Travis and Trevor in case they try railroading us?"

"Sure, Mom will be busy for at least another hour." After tucking the quilted heart into the pocket of my denim skirt, I followed him out the front door. A tiny spark of wanting and desire fluttered like a firefly, but I squashed it. "Isn't blood supposed to be thicker than water? Shouldn't you be plotting with your brothers against Mom and me?" His arm brushed against mine as I shifted closer to let another couple pass.

"I'm the middle child who has been gone for over twenty years. They have no allegiance to me. And you'd agree to anything that doesn't involve taking your mom back to the cities."

"Seems clear. You want the motorcycle, and I want to live alone. So, the question is, what do the others want?"

"Travis needs money. Dad mentioned he went through an expensive, messy divorce and has a girlfriend, but you didn't hear that from me." He lowered his eyebrows.

I inhaled the crisp night air. "I'm guessing she's the reason for his long hair, but I'm not here to judge. What they do with their lives is none of my business. What about Trevor?"

Ty grinned until crinkles appeared around his eyes. "He is desperate for Travis' approval and scared to death of your mom."

At the corner of Main and Pearl, the traffic light turned green. I stepped off the curb. "What's your plan?"

He grabbed my left hand.

I teetered on the curb before regaining my balance. I was about to shout, *what are you doing?* Then I noticed his still body and intense expression as he scanned the streets. The hairs on the back of my neck stood up. I tried to swallow as the pounding of my heart increased.

He signaled to the left with his eyes. "The squad car pulled behind the black sedan with no license plate and tinted windows. Cross the street." His grasp tightened.

"What's going on?"

"Potential drug bust or—" His steps quickened for a half block before stopping. "If the vehicle's occupants are involved in an illegal activity, they might shoot at the approaching officer. I want you safe." He pulled me close for a side hug.

"I never noticed the car." What if gunfire erupted? I could be dead. If Ty had worked for JR, he would have noticed the misappropriation of funds and saved the company.

"Hey, it's okay. Want to hear a fun fact?" He tilted his head and gave a goofy smile.

"Sure."

"Third Street has more bars than any other city in America."

"Seriously?" I glanced up and down the avenue at the neon lights.

"The information came from a reliable source."

"Let me guess, the bartender?"

He grinned.

The entire street glowed like a deserted nighttime carnival. Flashing bar signs with clever names and scrolling electronic window banners advertised daily drink specials.

I peered through the plate-glass window of Dew Drop Inn. A young man sat at the bar while the bartender stared at the large overhead TV. "Where is everyone? Do they all know something I don't?" Would there be a gang shoot-out?

"It's a college town."

His voice didn't sound strained, and his movements were relaxed.

"After finals, the students leave, and the tourists don't start flocking to the city until after Memorial Day."

Exhaling, I felt some of the tension drain from my shoulders. This was the same path I took earlier with Mom. I waved to the only other couple and wondered if they, too, were from The Club. The older woman had soft white curls, a blue-striped purse, and matching shoes.

She returned the wave with one hand while she tugged the hand of the man walking beside her.

The sight of them caused a pang deep in my stomach. They looked like an advertisement for growing old, happy, and content. But I reminded myself that a love life wasn't like playing the billion-dollar lottery. In dating, when you lose, you don't just crumple up the ticket. Sometimes, loving the wrong man screws up your whole life. Instead of a decent salary and money saved for your future, you work a dead-end job for less than twenty bucks an hour.

Attached to the soft glowing streetlights were oversized baskets with petunias and potato vines. By the end of summer, the bright-green vines would be trailing to the ground, and the red-white-and-blue flower heads would spill over the top.

Ty stopped in front of a paddlewheel boat and pointed to the ground.

I stooped and picked up the shiny dime. "Bernie, why did you leave me a motorcycle?" I flipped the cool coin between my fingers.

"A rhetorical question?"

"No." I held the dime higher.

"Before he passed, he told me someone had snuffed out your spark and hoped the motorcycle might rekindle your passion for life." Ty released my hand and brushed his fingers over his hair.

I slipped the coin into my pocket. *Bernie, thank you.* "Did you know he mailed me a birthday card with ten dollars inside every year? I loved that about your dad."

"My brothers and I also got a card with ten dollars. Everyone joked about Dad not keeping up with inflation. Now, I'd give anything to get another card this year." He slipped an arm around my shoulders.

The weight of his arm comforted and confused me. Would he kiss me again? Did I want a third kiss? The buzz of the phone caught my attention. "Sorry, I'd better get this. Probably Mom."

His arm fell away.

I retrieved the phone. Three texts from Mom. I read the last one.

—*Sal, I'm ready to go home. Do I need to find my own ride?*—

I respond before turning back to Ty. "You don't have to be the one to breathe life into me. Not sure if last night happened because you felt an obligation to your dad, guilt, or you're trying to get a certain real estate agent off your mind?"

"Amber doesn't occupy my thoughts. Last night, Travis demanded that I avoid you. Intrigued to see if my dad's assessment was right, I rushed over. After talking…" His voice softened as he leaned closer. "What would it take to spark your passion?"

I tensed and crossed my arms. "My co-worker Joe warned me about this after Wendy died and again before I left work on Friday."

With a furrowed brow, he tilted his head. "What?"

"*STERB.*"

He brushed a hand through his short hair. "The military has a lot of acronyms, but that's a new one."

"Walk me back, and I'll explain it." The warmth of his hand encased mine. "It stands for short-term energy relieving behavior because there is so much emotion with death. Sex is a great, quick way to release energy. After experiencing a loved one's death, some people have heightened desire, and others, of course, clean, cook, or climb mountains."

"Is that why I always see you doing dishes?"

"I hadn't thought about it. Flipping a house could

be your outlet."

He tilted his head. "Or you and I could find another way to release my energy."

"And I was just beginning to like you." I shook loose his hand and gave him a slight shove. "Do we have a plan for tomorrow's meeting?" A cool breeze ruffled the green leaves in the trees lining the street. Black wrought iron fencing encircled their little trunks and reminded me of my one trip to the zoo. I hated seeing the animals in cages.

"Any idea what your mom wants?"

I tapped a finger against my bottom lip. Her behavior seemed a little off. She always had a plan, but now, I couldn't figure out her endgame. "I know she hates being alone. So, a house full of people working would thrill her, and I'm sure she'll eventually want companionship. If I could find a place with a large senior population, I could get her to move. The last thing I want is to spend my weekends in River City."

"The quicker I can put River City in my rearview mirror, the happier I'll be, too. There is nothing here for me now that Dad has passed. So, I'll agree to let your mom stay until she finds accommodations if you consent to give me the motorcycle."

"Okay, but you'll need to pay me enough to cover the deposit, a few months' rent, and moving expenses. I have no idea what Mom's finances look like, but I'm barely making ends meet."

"Money isn't the problem. Twenty-eight thousand, no flipping the house, and no Amber." He grasped my hand.

I sighed, wishing he sealed the deal with a kiss instead of a handshake.

Chapter Four

On Sunday morning, I walked into Mom's bedroom and felt my nostrils pinch shut. The space smelled like a defunct thrift store, with dust, remnants of cheap perfume, and body odor. "You need fresh air." I pushed the heavy drapes aside and yanked the wooden window frame. "It's stuck."

Mom groaned, swung her feet onto the hardwood floor, and tugged a short nightie over her bare bottom. "It sticks."

After a few whacks, the window opened. Travis was right. She needed a more manageable place to live. "It's a little after nine. The boys are coming over to discuss the next step, and I'm heading home. I've got things to do."

She plopped onto the edge of her bed. "It's not the things you have to do. It's the thing you don't want to do. I saw how you two looked at each other in the bar. You deserve fun, but Ty's a heartbreaker. He's got all the moves, probably a woman in all fifty states. So, unless you want to be Ms. Wisconsin, stay away."

The sound of the front door opening and footsteps echoed outside her door.

"Guess they're here early. I'll start some coffee while you get dressed." I walked into the kitchen and flashed a wave. "She'll be out in a minute. I'll put some coffee on, and I hope you brought breakfast."

Travis shook his red curls. "Trevor and I stopped earlier to eat, but Ty mentioned he'd bring food. Kind of thought he'd be here by now."

Mom stepped into the kitchen still in her nightie, her hair sticking up like a troll doll and eyes like a raccoon. "No sense getting dressed. This shouldn't take long." She screwed up her face and circled the table before sitting. "Where's Ty and the food?"

I leaned against the counter, listening to the coffeepot sputter, and watched Mom stare at Trevor, who squirmed like a toddler.

When the front door banged open, Trevor flew off his chair. "I'll see if he needs help."

"Morning," Ty's voice rang out. He swung a large white paper bag onto the table. "Trevor, get the plates and cups."

He scrambled to do Ty's bidding, pulling the dishes from the cupboard. He set out three plates and five cups.

"Well, Mrs. Ridel, I have the best breakfast sandwiches." The paper crinkled as Ty reached inside. He placed sandwiches on the plates and packets of hot sauce on the table.

I poured coffee for everyone. "Hopefully, no one needs cream or sugar."

Trevor jumped up. "Should be some in the refrigerator. Dad and I always liked creamer." He grinned.

The scent of bacon, cheese, and egg mingled with the fragrant, fresh-brewed coffee. I settled a hand on my rumbling stomach and unwrapped the stuffed English muffin. Cheese oozed out the sides. I took a bite. The slightly tangy bread, creamy cheddar, and variety of seasonings created a perfect combination. I nodded my approval to Ty.

Mom dissected her sandwich and examined each item before putting everything back together.

Did she not trust Ty?

Ty pointed between his brothers. "Dig in, I brought enough for everyone."

Trevor widened his smile, and between the black bushy beard, his white teeth appeared as he poured creamer, turning the black coffee off-white. "Trevor took me to breakfast." He grinned at Ty like a dog waiting for a treat.

"So." Mom waved her sandwich. "Let's not play games. The vote is going to be three to two or four to two. Looks like you'll be staying, Ty, if you want the bike."

"Let's vote. All in favor of listing the house as is." Ty raised his hand.

Trevor slowly raised his arm.

Icy fingers clasped my wrist. Mom shook my arm so hard that the bacon and cheese slid off the egg and onto the plate.

"Sally, you know, I don't mind the cities. If they list the house, then I'll move in with you. Just give me thirty minutes to pack my suitcase, roomie."

Ty lowered his arm. "It's okay, Mabel—"

"It's still Mrs. Ridel to you."

Ty leaned forward, resting on his elbows. "I'll agree to you staying in the house until you find an apartment. I'll pay twenty-five for the bike. You'll make the same money. And no one will work in the heat and mosquitoes. It's a win-win."

Mom wagged an index finger as she lowered her

penciled-in eyebrows to mere slits. "Who wants to flip the house and double their profit for a little labor? Sal, just think you and me roomies, or you give up a few weekends."

"Sal." Ty reached across the table for my hand. "She's bluffing. If you don't raise your hand, I'll give you thirty-two for the bike."

Travis sighed, his curls obscuring both eyes. "Sal, I'm serious. As soon as there's an offer, Mabel's on the street." He pointed at Trevor. "Lower your hand if you don't want Mabel living on the streets."

Sweat leaked from every pore on my body. This was worse than testifying against JR. I watched Ty mouth the word, *bluffing*. The ticking of the kitchen wall clock echoed. Unlike being in the courthouse, nothing was keeping me here. I stood and started for the front door.

Mom rushed ahead and blocked the door. "You're not running away." She planted her hands on her hips. "Sit back down and vote."

Planting my feet, I closed my eyes, thinking of options as her body pressed against mine.

"Trevor!" Mom's voice crashed past my ears like a shotgun shell. "Your daddy would be so disappointed. Kicking me to the curb. He always had a soft spot for you. Said of the three boys, you had the biggest, kindest heart. Guess he was wrong."

"Stop." I turned.

Trevor paled and, with the deer-in-the-headlights look, stared at Mom.

Ty shook his head, sighing as he slouched.

Travis flashed a toothy smile and bobbed his head of curls.

If Trevor caved, he'd lose all of Ty's respect, and a big wedge would be driven between their fragile bonds. I turned toward Mom. Couldn't she see how this bickering wasn't good?

She winked and nodded.

None of this made sense. Was she up to something?

"Let's vote." Travis rubbed his hands together. "So, little Trevor, should we list the house and toss Mabel—"

"Stop!" I spun and glared at Travis. "Fine." The word hung like a limp white flag being waved. "I'll help you with the house, but as soon as I find Mom an apartment, list the house, and give the bike to Ty."

"Nope." Mom nudged me. "Ty only gets the bike if he stays and helps."

This wasn't the first time someone had pushed me into a corner. If I refused to help and they listed the house, I'd end up with Mom living with me and six months to get a motorcycle license. I walked back to the table and sat without looking across the table at Ty. What if I couldn't pass the test or if she got comfortable living with me and didn't want to move? What about Ty? Didn't he deserve to have his dad's motorcycle? I took a sip of my coffee, put the egg back into the sandwich, and took another bite, finding comfort in the food.

Mom plopped into the chair. "Well."

I took another bite and finally looked over at Ty. "This is good. Did you make them?"

"Nope, bought them at Ma's Kitchen. She showed me how to freeze them and how to warm them up—" He smiled.

Travis stood. His curls bounced as he started pacing around the table. "I suppose next, you'll want to talk about laundry. Some of us have places to go. So, do I call Amber and tell her to pound in the *for sale* sign, or do we devise a plan?"

Mom took a big slurp of coffee, pursed her lips, and sputtered, "Is this tea?"

"How big is this motorcycle?" I finished my sandwich and considered taking another one but decided against it. The way the day started. I'd need the comfort of an ice cream cone later.

"Come on." Ty stood. "I'll show you the cycle. And you don't need to drive this one. All you need is to get a motorcycle endorsement."

"So, I don't have to drive."

Travis stomped over in a blur of red curls. "Yes, you do. They'll make you weave in and out of cones and avoid obstacles, and they'll fail you if you crash the bike or put your foot down on the course. Go look. It's big and heavy."

Shifting my gaze between the two, I stood. *Is Travis trying to scare me? Could the bike crush me?* Dragging my feet, I followed Ty out the back door, and waited for him to unlock the garage door. I made the mistake of peering into his ocean-blue eyes. The urge to give in to Ty was overwhelming, but I didn't want Mom as a roommate. For a month or two, he'd be inconvenienced, but living with Mom could turn into a life sentence.

He shoved open the white wooden door with the small pane cracked window. A big, shiny red motorcycle stood in the center of the crumbling concrete floor.

"The bike is the size of a compact car. How much does the thing weigh?"

"Eight hundred pounds."

"I'm not even sure I can still bench press eighty pounds." Hopes of getting Mom a place of her own fluttered away like a moth to a flame.

Ty rested his hands on my shoulders. "Sal, you can do this. All you need is a motorcycle license. You are strong, brave, and don't want a roommate."

The heat from his touch warmed my shoulders. *Could I believe his skewed assessment?* He was right about my motivation, but did I have courage? I shook my head.

"I spoke with the lawyer. He's also a board member and the treasurer for The Club. He told me if you don't get a motorcycle endorsement, then the bike gets donated for a raffle prize."

"What if you bought all the tickets?"

"Nope. The only way to guarantee I get the bike is for you to get an endorsement."

Threading fingers through my hair, I tilted my head back, and sighed. "Great. Added pressure."

"Climb on the back and get a feel for it." Ty straddled the bike.

Standing with hands on my hips, I noticed orange hair appear in the doorway, followed by Travis.

"Please," Ty cooed.

Mom glared, shaking her head and mouthing the words, *don't do it.*

"Fine." I scampered behind him and tried not to think about my legs spread wide and him sitting inches away.

He scooted back.

Through my denim jeans, I could feel the heat of his hips. Of course, sitting behind Ty wasn't like driving the motorcycle. I leaned closer and whispered, "You know I'm going to vote with Mom. I hate when she wins, but I'll get the endorsement and give you the bike. They can't make you stay."

The only acknowledgment he heard my words was a slight nod.

Sitting behind Ty, I couldn't keep my imagination from going wild. Suddenly, I wanted to feel the wind blowing in my face and watch mountain streams, herds of bison, and majestic pine trees flash past. I shivered. Nothing good came from staying here daydreaming. "I've got to go. Guess I'll see you next weekend."

Our audience grumbled and walked away.

Instead of rushing after them, I lingered.

Ty showed me the basics, brakes, and throttle before inclining his head toward the service door. "Come on. Let's watch Travis and your mom gloat over their victory and spare Trevor an ulcer worrying about whose side to choose." He twisted and sideways hugged me. "Nice thing you did for him. Thank you."

"You're welcomed."

He looped an arm around my waist. "If you weren't leaving, then I would have taken you for a ride."

"Hmmm," slipped between my slacked lips as my body went from tense to supple. If only I hadn't told the little white lie about needing to leave. A motorcycle ride sounded like fun. I walked back to the house with his arm around me. Did he want them to see our strength and to think of us as a team? Or did he like me?

After agreeing to help, I watched Mom and Travis congratulate each other with fist bumps. Shaking my head, I gathered the backpack from the floor and waved goodbye. I heard footsteps behind me, turned, and spotted Ty. *Awe.* He's walking me to my car. I could feel my steps lighten as nervousness bubbled in my stomach. Would he kiss me? On the curb, beneath the overhanging branches of the Ginkgo tree, I opened the rear hatchback.

Ty picked my backpack up from the boulevard.

Leaning closer, I wanted to feel his arm wrap around me. Time ticked by, but he didn't reach for me. Should I make the second move?

He reached over and set the bag in the trunk.

I wet my lips.

"See you next weekend."

What the fudge? I clenched my hands. "Yeah."

He rushed over and opened the driver's door.

I lingered between him and the seat, giving him another chance.

He stepped back.

Planting my bottom on the driver's seat, I yanked the seatbelt around me. He knew I didn't have a choice about the vote. Was he using me only to get the motorcycle?

****

On Monday, I drove into Smith and Son's Heating and Cooling complex. The parking lot had a hundred white vans with company logos, a warehouse and shop the size of two football fields, and an administrative building that had once been a fast-food restaurant. Sometimes, I swore you could still smell French fries and onions. The staff had no public contact, so most of the office employees wore jeans and leggings, but not Joe, the company accountant. Today, he hovered by the door in Italian designer slacks, linen shirt, and leather loafers. Unlike me, Joe enjoyed coming to work, whereas I only wanted the largest cup of coffee and a paycheck.

I brushed past him in my tummy control, black yoga pants and a dark navy tunic top. "As always, an uneventful weekend. How about you? Yardwork?" Without waiting for his answer, I walked past my cubicle and into the small kitchen with white-tiled walls, a coffee machine, a dorm-size refrigerator, a table with five chairs, and a small sink with a sign stating *all employees must wash their hands*, probably left over from when the place had teenagers frying burgers.

Most employees spent their days working out of their trucks or in the warehouse, and less than a dozen people worked in the administrative building.

I spotted Joe leaning against the door frame. I braced myself before opening the refrigerator. Nothing popped out, but his lunch was on the third shelf where I always put mine. People thought I could not change because I like the consistency, but the change wasn't an issue. I put my lunch on the second shelf and assumed he had moved my coffee cup from its typical spot. Sure enough, after opening two cabinet doors, I found the mug. With a steamy cup of coffee, I stepped from the kitchenette, smiled at Joe, and started toward my workstation.

"You seem different."

I plopped into the desk chair and switched on my computer. "I'm the same."

"Something happened this weekend?"

The other customer service representatives were already at stations, wearing leggings and T-shirts. Most were under twenty-one and didn't stay a year before leaving. I envied their flexibility and free spirit attitude. I picked up my headphones and smiled at them, but no one acknowledged me.

"Come on," Joe sang the words. "Tell me, pretty please."

I motioned for him to come closer. "I kissed my stepbrother Ty on the mouth." A wave of sadness engulfed me. I wanted to share the story with Wendy—the only person who'd hire me after JR's name made headlines for fraud and embezzlement. Being both the office manager and the felon's fiancée had prospective employers questioning my innocence.

Again, I cursed fate for robbing me of Wendy and my father while JR only had to serve three years. The man wrecked so many lives. He was the sole reason I was at a dead-end job for the next eighteen years, which seemed more like being on death row than having my freedom.

Joe rubbed his hands together. "Don't leave me hanging? How was lip-locking with your brother?"

"The best kiss of my life." I sighed, plugged in the headphones, and pretended to focus on scheduling work orders. In a month, the days would fly by as the temperatures soared and people found out their air conditioning units were no longer working. But today, instead of placing customers on hold, I wished the phone would ring.

With nothing to keep me busy, I searched the Internet for apartments in River City. A luxury apartment popped onto the screen. The building was close to The Club, with a parking ramp and security. With the money from selling the bike, I could subsidize the cost. I texted Mom the information and suggested she call.

My next search for houses for sale in River City sent me down a rabbit hole, and I found Amber. She was a successful agent with twenty years in the business and no mention of a husband or family. What kind of history did she have with Ty? And why was he holding a grudge after all these years when everyone else seemed to like her? Not finding any answers online, I wound my way to motorcycle classes. Reading through the class description, I turned and spotted Joe hovering over my shoulder.

"What are you working on?" He leaned closer to the monitor and shook his head. "Let's grab lunch?"

In the small administrative lunchroom, I explained the situation. "Ty offered me twenty-eight thousand if I could get a motorcycle endorsement."

Joe nodded. "So, when do the classes start?

"They have several five-day sessions with options, but—"

"Hey, hey." Lisa rushed in, wearing an emerald-green *V*-neck sweater, matching colored earrings, and eye shadow. She started working here after high school and was only a few years from retirement. "How was the weekend?" She slid into the chair, pushing her vibrant red hair from her face. "They say deaths come in threes. Who's next?"

Joe gestured with his hands. "She kissed her brother on the mouth."

"I didn't know who Ty was—"

"She liked it." Joe peeled back the plastic wrap from his sandwich.

Lisa clicked her tongue. "I thought your mom lived with this guy for years. How could you not know Ty was your brother?"

"Almost stepbrother." I paused and pointed an index finger. "Do you have a pierced tongue?"

Lisa nodded. "Yeah, got it done after Wendy died. Next month, I'm getting a tattoo."

"Wow. I can't believe you didn't tell me. Did it hurt?"

"Get back to the story." Joe flapped his arms.

Nodding, I couldn't tear my gaze from Lisa. Since Wendy passed, the bravest thing I'd done was occasionally try a new fruit or vegetable. *How can I live for someone else if I'm not living for myself?*

Joe tapped his right foot. "Enough of a dramatic pause."

Sighing, I repeated how Ty had retired from the military. The Old Fashioned mulled my brain, and I'd need to drive back every weekend. Forcing the curve from my smile, I tried to sound depressed. "I'll probably have to see him again."

Lisa propped her elbows on the table and batted her lashes. "You should have a summer romance. They're the best. All the heat and passion." She slowly peeled her banana. "It's been a few years. I'm not sure I could handle three months, but maybe a cruise for singles. A week at sea and then kiss them goodbye." She bit the top of the banana.

After peeling the kiwi, I took a tentative bite and tried to decide whether to swallow or spit the thing out.

Joe dabbed his lips with a paper napkin. "What are

you doing?"

I sneered at the green fruit with tiny black seeds. "You know, living for Wendy. Trying new things."

"Wendy would want you to do a cruise or at least your stepbrother." Lisa popped the top on her diet soda. "She detested kiwis."

"Yeah," Joe said. "Either choice would be safer than driving a motorcycle."

"Let's change the subject." I pushed the fruit back into my lunch bag.

Lisa picked up her can. "If you're not interested in a summer fling, you could give him my number."

Struggling to swallow, I shook my head. Was the fuzzy feeling coming from the thought of Lisa with Ty or an allergic reaction to the fruit?

"A fling is what you need. Think of him as a gateway to dating again." Joe twisted off the top of his water bottle.

"No." I paused long enough to make eye contact. "I'm not a princess with a happily ever after. I'm the chick with warts from kissing toads."

"So, you're saying you have a disastrous track record?"

"Don't listen to him." Lisa wagged a finger. "Keep kissing toads. There must be more to life than work and holing up in your apartment. You're not getting any younger."

Taking a sip of the flavor-enhanced water, I cringed. "The only thing I have left is my heart, and no way will I gift wrap it for a man with women all over the country."

Joe tossed the wrapper from his deli sandwich into the garbage. "JR's the one who's in jail, but you live like you're in prison. Almost like you're guilty. You weren't involved, were you?"

"No!" I abruptly stood. The chair legs scrapped across the floor. "As soon as I noticed a suspicious transaction, I questioned JR. He twisted my words, and suddenly, I was on the defense. He had explanations for everything. Until the day I caught him altering a surety bond. I pretended not to notice but afterward called in an anonymous tip." I crumpled the lunch bag and blinked twice. "This looks exactly like a heart."

"If she sees the Virgin Mary or the man on the moon in her coffee cup, let me know." Joe winked.

Lisa giggled. "I watched a TV show where a guy saw faces in random objects. It's called pareidolia."

Sighing, I tossed the heart in the trash, and returned to my desk. Late in the afternoon, after a quick run to the restroom, I returned to my workstation and found a dozen *Get Out Of Jail Free* slips of paper decorated with tiny red hearts tossed across my desk. I turned and spotted Joe and Lisa fifty feet away, giggling.

Shaking my head and performing a dramatic eye roll, I mouthed, *Thanks.* This summer, I'd start living.

Chapter Five

On Friday evening, instead of relaxing, I packed my car and texted Mom I was on the way.

She responded with a screenshot.

—*Tell Sally she'll need a mask, gloves, goggles, and safety shoes.*—

A phone number with Mom's area code, but no name appeared at the top of the image. Apparently, she wasn't giving Ty my contact information? I thought about texting her but sent a happy face emoji instead.

****

Three and a half hours later, I exited the vehicle with my weekend backpack and two boxes of new boots. With an hour before sunset, the temperatures were just beginning to cool, but after a long, cold winter anything above sixty seemed warm. I stepped into the living room and gasped. The furniture was draped with plastic, and the hole in the wall now looked like a doorway.

Mom came from the kitchen, wearing one-piece white overalls with rolled-up sleeves.

This was the first time I saw her without cleavage. A navy bandana covered her hair, and she looked a bit like the woman from the World War II posters.

"You need to put your stuff back in your car. The dust gets everywhere. I've got an extra overall you can wear. Ty should return in fifteen minutes."

I followed the instructions and met her in the bedroom.

She swiped a hand across her forehead. "You're going to want to take off your jeans and T-shirt. I'm sweating like a hormonal woman at a male strip club. You got boots?"

"Was the screenshot a message from Ty?"

"Yeah, he's a stickler for safety, but I'm not complaining. He's a hard worker." Mom leaned closer. "I know I told you to keep your distance. But now, I need you to distract him and slow him down. If he keeps up this pace, the house will be ready to list in three weeks. I don't want to move to Minneapolis with you—"

"Hello." A deep, masculine voice echoed outside the door.

The baritone voice increased my heart rate as a warm rush wrapped my body like a hug. *Ty.*

"One minute." Mom gestured. "Hurry, change, and don't forget what we discussed."

Sidetrack him? How? I slipped into the jumpsuit, pulled on the boots, ran my fingers through my hair, and ambled into the kitchen. I looked like a cowboy from a Western movie, but instead of being fit, I resembled a giant marshmallow man.

Wearing cargo shorts and a dark T-shirt with a bar logo covered in dust, he leaned against the sink

"Hey, big news. I am signing up for motorcycle lessons."

"Sal, you know that saying and doing are two different things."

I pushed the confusion over his reaction aside as tension pursed my lips. "You're grumpy. I need a helmet, goggles, and my next paycheck to pay for the course. I used my mad fund to buy boots."

He glanced at my footwear, cocked his right eyebrow, and gave a slight chin nod.

Whoever said women were moody hadn't met Ty. "Mom mentioned you had something you needed me to do."

"Let's wait until morning?" He brushed a hand across his hair.

"Great idea." Mom's enthusiastic nod dislodged the scarf from her head. "Sal must be tired from driving and working all week. See you kids, tomorrow, but not too early."

"Wait." I held a hand in front of Mom. "Where are you going?"

"Nowhere." She winked. "The spare bedroom is a mess with construction materials. I figured you'd be more comfortable at the trailer, but if you want, we can share a bed."

I shifted my gaze between the two of them.

"Makes no difference to me where you sleep." Ty shrugged.

So, this is how she wanted me to distract him? I stomped down the hall and into the bedroom.

She followed closely. "Don't look so sour. Remember the saying about honey?"

"This is a mistake." I tugged the zipper down.

"Nonsense. Besides, I took your advice. The downtown apartment is perfect. Lidia and Paul live there, and Francis is also on the waitlist. The office gal thought there'd be a couple of openings late this fall or early winter. I filled out the application and paid the deposit."

"Great, but no way am I—"

"Of course, you're not." She pointed toward the door. "Go get changed. He's waiting."

Fifteen minutes later, I stepped from the bedroom and flashed Ty a sarcastic smile. "Show me to my pumpkin?"

"Huh?" He narrowed his gaze.

"Campers always remind me of the nursery rhyme about the guy who kept his wife in a pumpkin."

Ty curled his lip and flashed a sideways glance. "Put your stuff in my truck. We'll leave your car here."

I retrieved my backpack without squabbling over the lack of the word *please*. The oversized, super-duty, blue pickup had no running boards. After two failed attempts, I found a handhold and climbed into the bucket seat.

Ty sat in the driver's seat, tapping four fingers on the steering wheel.

I cringed at his double-eye roll. "Nice."

"Thanks."

He had missed the sarcasm in my response, but I heard the strain in his voice and leaned over the large center console to listen.

"Bought *the beast* to pull the camper. Dad and I planned to travel the country. Instead…"

As his words trailed off, I rested a palm on his right forearm. "I'm sorry. Bernie told me about the trip. A big adventure to see all the national parks. And now, instead of enjoying a summer with your dad…" I swallowed. How could I be so self-absorbed not to notice Ty's loss? "I'm sorry about all this." I made a sweeping gesture to encompass the mess of remodeling the house.

He didn't nod or speak as he drove across the blue suspension bridge onto the large island that split the Mississippi into channels.

Wisconsin claimed the no-named section of land, but if you followed the highway west for three miles, you'd end up in a small town in Minnesota, which claimed to be the world's apple capital.

He pulled off the highway and into the crowded River Day Resort parking lot. Besides a campground, the property included an event center for wedding venues, a store, a restaurant, and a bar. Ty crept the truck toward the campground entrance. The setting sun highlighted everything outside the windshield in hues of oranges and yellows. Driving through the gate, he avoided a large wedding party, kids on bikes, and a golf cart decorated like a Tiki Bar.

"This is like a massive bash." Music came from all directions, punctuated with laughter, hollering, kids squealing, and horns honking.

"The locals tell me that the weekends are busy until midnight. But during the week, the park is quiet. I hadn't planned on staying…"

Watching him focus his attention on the pedestrians and golf cart traffic, I kept another apology to myself.

He crept forward and punched his code into a keypad labeled *campers and guests only*. The mechanical arm inched open. He drove down the road and pointed. "The log-sided building to the left has bathrooms and showers. The red building next door is the laundry room."

I cringed and made a mental note of the location. This was going to be a long weekend. Why did anyone want to go camping?

The campground was a tangle of roads, cottonwoods, maples, oaks, and pines. He drove past a stack of canoes and a children's play area with half a dozen kids. The campsites were haphazard. Instead of neat rows, campers parked between mature trees, and no two campsites were alike. The trees, roads, and river channels dictated the spaces. Some campers were old and small, with wooden decks built around them. Others were large and newer, but they all had yard art, plants, rugs, and chairs.

After ten minutes of crawling down the dirt road, Ty stopped, shifted into Reverse, and began backing.

The truck alarm beeped insistently.

I gripped the door handle harder and braced for impact.

The beeping stopped.

I glanced over and saw his quick grin.

The first smile I had seen from Ty today and the slight gesture boosted my mood. He was slightly cocky, a bit broken, and I wanted to fix him. Did Bernie feel this way when he gifted me the bike?

"You seem surprised I didn't hit the camper."

"I had no idea the truck would fit under the camper, and the noise kept getting louder. You didn't hit it, did you?"

He laughed as he pushed open his door. "Let me show you the pumpkin."

"More like a mansion," I mumbled.

"I heard that."

Ty stood at the bottom of the camper steps with my backpack. He unlocked the door and ushered me inside.

I stood, looking at the high ceilings, expansive

living room, and built in wood cabinets and granite countertops. "This isn't a camper. It's an apartment on wheels."

"Kitchen, dinette, and entertainment." He stood in the doorway and pointed.

"A TV, stove, and sink." This was nothing like I imagined. Modern farmhouse style in gray, teal-blue, and charcoal.

"You think this is nice? Let me show you your bedroom."

I followed him up two steps. The bathroom had a large walk-in shower and a skylight. "A toilet and running water, Phew. I thought I'd have to go down the road to use the restroom."

"That's why you moaned when I pointed out the bathhouse. Come on, I'll show you to the bedroom." He pushed open the pocket door.

I shook my head at the sight of the queen-size bed and the teal bedspread with matching pillows. The room wasn't large, but you could walk around the bed.

He flipped a switch and the lights in the ceiling dimmed.

"Whoa. I thought there would be bunk beds or a couple of cots. I'm not Ms. Wisconsin."

Ty grasped my shoulders with his right eyebrow cocked higher than his left. "What are you talking about?"

"I didn't mean to say that out loud. Mom said you had a woman in every state, and you're looking for Wisconsin." I stared into his blue eyes and felt myself getting lost.

He inched closer, and a slow smile creased his face. "I don't remember asking you to hook up."

"What would have given me that impression?" I rested a hand on his chest to keep us separated. "Must have been the melting and moaning when I kissed you." He smelled like apples and crisp fall days. I could feel my brain shutting down as I leaned toward him.

"Sal—"

The sound of knocking stifled my movements. He didn't say shacking up but with only one bed...*Did his gaze soften? He's licking his lips.* The pounding in my chest increased. I'm almost fifty. I'm not getting any younger. A couple of weeks, and he'll be a distant blur in the sunset. I leaned closer but refused to make the first move.

"Ty," a voice called. "I know you're home."

"I don't think they're going away." He stepped back.

I followed him down the two steps, and when he shifted toward the door, I walked around the center island with the large farm sink. On the right side of the island was the kitchen with a refrigerator, stove, microwave, and an entertainment center with a large TV. A small kitchen booth and a loveseat were on the left side of the island, and a back wall held a door.

Ty opened the main door.

Taking a dozen steps toward the mystery door, I peeked inside and felt heat singe my cheeks. Another bedroom. This one was much smaller and had a double bed. I stepped inside. Ty's clothes hung on a rod, with his shoes in a neat row below.

"Two bedrooms," I mumbled. Why doesn't he want to sleep with me? I'm not that old, and he liked the way I kissed.

"Sal?"

I stepped from the room.

"The neighbors invited us for a fish fry and a beer."

"You have two bedrooms. I thought—" I tugged the damp T-shirt from my abs.

His fingers brushed lightly across my forearm. "Let's go next door."

The cool night air did little to remove the heat from my cheeks. Hopefully, a cold one would help me forget.

Ty carried two bright-blue, folded lawn chairs with price tags still attached across the lawn to a smaller version fifth wheel camper. "Wayne and Barb, I'd like you to meet Sal."

The couple was older. Wayne looked like a lead singer in an old-time country band, and Barb looked like the sweetest of grandmothers with long snow-white braided hair.

She rushed forward and embraced me. "I hope you like fish. They've been biting all week."

For a short, stout woman, she was strong. I patted her back. "Sounds delicious. What can I do to help?"

After hugging Ty, she ushered me toward their camper.

Inside, I watched her gather paper plates and napkins.

She loaded my arms with plastic containers from the refrigerator and another from the cupboard. "If you could set the bowls on the picnic table. I'll be outside in a minute. Have Wayne grab you a beer from the cooler." Barb motioned toward the screen door before heading up the two stairs to the bathroom.

Balancing the load, I freed my right hand, but couldn't find a doorknob. I pressed my hip against the white metal door, but it didn't open. Outsmarted by a trailer door. I got ready to call out to Barb.

Ty appeared on the other side. "I figured you might need some help."

"Apparently. You'll have to show me how these doors work."

"If you ask nice." He winked. "I might even teach you how to empty the waste tanks."

Wayne laughed. "I'll teach you to dump mine, too."

"Sorry, Ty already has my weekend planned."

Wayne jabbed Ty.

"Yep, we'll both be sore before tomorrow is over."

The light, flirty, teasing side of Ty warmed me. The invitation for beers had been a needed distraction. He seemed to relax while being outdoors.

The assortment of pan fish was delicious, the fire welcoming, and the beers cold. Casting a sideways glance, I made eye contact with Ty and the Ms. Wisconsin incident no longer shamed me.

He slid closer.

Could he read my mind? Once, I had gone with Wendy to a psychic, and the woman explained thoughts were nothing more than electrical impulses and that bones and skin were not the best insulators. She claimed to hear the noise people generated.

I fixed my gaze on his features and concentrated. *Can I hear his thoughts?*

After a swig of beer, his tongue slowly swiped his bottom lip.

Hopefully, he couldn't read mine.

He raised his bottle. "To good friends."

Long necks clinked, and the cool beer tasted like a perfect summer.

"To friends and campfires."

Last Friday, like tonight, he was a magnet pulling me toward fun. Could he add some spark back to my life? The two of us could enjoy the summer together, and in the fall, he could send an occasional text with photos of the places he's been.

As the sun faded, I scooted my chair closer to the fire. Voices mingled, logs crackled, and from a speaker, the sounds from Dolly Parton and Kenny Rogers singing "Islands in the Stream."

Ty and Wayne began singing along. "…something to me…"

A golf cart drove past and beeped, and the men lowered their voices.

I raised my beer bottle, not wanting to think of Ty serenading me. "To my first night camping, or I guess a better term would be glamping."

More clinking and sipping.

"So, how did you meet?" Barb nudged me.

Ty leaned forward and wrapped an arm around my shoulders. "Picked her up at my dad's funeral dinner."

Wayne laughed. "Met my bride in prison."

"What?" I narrowed my gaze. "Criminals? No way."

Smirking, Barb bobbed her head. "Yep, Wayne is a thief. He stole my heart while we worked at the same prison, but that was long ago."

Twenty minutes later, Wayne and Ty smothered the fire, and I declined their offer to go fishing first thing in the morning.

After walking back and stepping into Ty's glamper, I turned, swaying a bit. "Hey, earlier, I didn't mean to imply you expected to sleep with me."

He brushed an index finger to my lips. "Shhhh. It's late, and we're both tired."

"Are you trying to tell me you're not interested?"

"I'd kiss you, but one kiss wouldn't be enough." He stepped back.

"And you don't want either of us waking up with regrets."

"Not me, but you might. I'm not the easiest guy. Civilian life is a big adjustment, and I can't promise anything but a memorable night."

No teasing or merriment crossed his stern features. But the beer had softened me. "Just one night, huh?"

"Good night, Sal. See you in the morning."

I watched him leave. So many things popped into my mind. But if he was only offering one evening, I didn't want this to be the one.

Snuggled between the clean sheets, I thought about Ty. Mom would be disappointed. Instead of distracting him from getting the house ready to sell, I would help him and get the motorcycle endorsement. He deserved to get out of town and start his big adventure. If I had realized how much of a sacrifice he was making with the constant reminders of his dad passing and losing their time together, I would have taken Mom to Minneapolis.

Instead of months, Ty only got a few weeks. If only Bernie had lived. Life seemed so unfair, and here I was, complaining about Mom living with me.

****

The following day, I woke to the blinding sun streaming through the window. I blinked and oriented myself to my location. Ty's mini mansion on wheels. I sniffed. *Coffee.* Faster than a quick-change artist, I descended the two steps in shorts and a tank top.

Ty sat at the small kitchen booth and nodded toward a coffee machine on the island and a bowl of pods. "Cups are in the cupboard. I don't have cream, but milk is in the refrigerator."

"Thanks." With a steamy cup of coffee, I slid across from Ty. The sweet scent of vanilla wafted from the cup as I blew across the top. Taking a tentative sip, I tasted the sweet and mild nuttiness of the brew without the overpowering coffee taste. "This is good."

"Can you cook?" He glanced up from his phone.

"Of course."

He nodded and went back to reading.

I stood and rummaged around in the kitchen, finding everything I needed. The assortment of fresh vegetables and the array of spices surprised me. I figured he had salt and ketchup as his only condiments. Thirty minutes later, I slid a spinach omelet down in front of Ty and again sat across from him with my plate of food.

He set his phone aside. "Wow. Looks delicious and smells good, too."

"The reason I'm so good at washing dishes is because I know how to cook. When you have a refrigerator full of food and a drawer full of spices, whipping a meal together is easy. You must cook?"

He shook his head and murmured an approval before taking another bite. "I do the basics, like sandwiches, and salads. Occasionally, a fried egg and toast. My dad could cook, and I had hoped he'd teach me on our trip. I bought the spices for him."

"Ty. I hate you got stuck in River City." I slipped my hand across the table. Something about him moved me. This was how I imagined I'd feel when I found the perfect canine companion. I'd just know, except Ty didn't want to be brought home, and he wanted to roam. "If you leave, I'll contact you when I get the motorcycle title. And if Travis kicks Mom out, I'll let her whip his butt and then figure out the next step."

He captured my extended hand. "You're full of surprises. Can I ask why the change of heart?"

"No reason other than you're a nice guy."

"After today, you'll change your mind. And as tempting as your offer is, I still have all this pent-up emotion and restless energy. Unless you have some other ideas." He released my hand.

"You could wash the dishes."

His laughter rumbled the dinette table.

This would be a wonderful summer. One memorable night. I grinned. Maybe Lisa was right about summer romance being the best.

Chapter Six

At five o'clock, I stepped from Mom's house, having accumulated over 10,000 steps from hauling busted plaster to the dumpster. I imagined my arms resembled overcooked spaghetti noodles from holding up drywall. I stood beside the passenger door of Ty's truck. "A little help."

He walked over. "What's up?"

"I don't think I can get inside. Everything aches."

"Reach up, and I'll give you a boost."

I grabbed the dash and panic handle as I felt his hands on my hips, and somehow, I slid into the black leather bucket seat. I glanced down. "You were right. I don't think you're so nice."

A moment later, he hopped into the driver's seat, showing no ill effects from a day of manual labor. Heading down the street, Ty glanced over. "I guess cooking dinner is out of the question."

"I don't even think I could lift an egg."

"Think you could lift a beer?"

I struggled to lift my heavy arm. "I'll ask for a straw." Casting a sideways glance, I caught his smile. He got my humor.

"Okay, I know a great place for beer and burgers."

"Sounds good." Something about him buying me dinner, because I was tired, made me feel cared for...I yawned. After trying to keep my eyes open, I rested them momentarily.

"Hey, sleepyhead." A warm hand brushed my shoulder.

Ty's voice cut through my drowsiness. I peered to the left through my partially opened eyes. The driver's seat was empty. The truck wasn't moving. I fumbled to get out of the seatbelt, shifted to the right, and sighed as Ty appeared beside my opened door. Behind him, I saw a river but no camper. "How long have I been asleep?"

"Almost an hour. I stopped and picked up something to eat. Hungry?"

"Starved. Thank you."

"No problem." He placed his hands around my waist, easing me to the ground.

"Hmm, besides being considerate." I grasped his left bicep and gave a squeeze. "You're strong."

"At the end of the summer, you'll be helping me out of the truck with all the muscles you're building."

"I was hoping the heavy lifting was all done." As I walked beside him, I brushed against his thigh.

"Are you that tired?"

"How much farther?"

He pointed toward the left.

Nestled between two trees, I spotted a picnic table facing the banks of the murky brown river. A fishing boat bobbed beside an island as a large boat sped past. "Where are we?"

"About forty-five minutes south of River City. It's a small park I found while driving. I like to come here to think. Someday, you can drive me down here on your motorcycle."

I shook my head. I couldn't imagine holding the bike with me on it, let alone both of us. But straddling a motorcycle and hanging onto Ty made me smile. I plopped onto the bench.

He set out paper-wrapped sandwiches, containers of potato salad, coleslaw, pickles, two paper plates, and bottles of water before sitting.

Quickly unfolding the paper, I glanced at the ham piled high between two slices of rye bread. "This isn't a burger."

"With the way you were snoring, I didn't want to upset the patrons at the bar—"

I couldn't remember when someone looked at me like I was decent, funny, and desirable. Before taking my first bite, I glanced at the sky, silently expressing my gratitude for meeting Ty.

With a full stomach, I gathered our wrappers and lumbered to the trash.

Ty put down the tailgate, grasped my waist, and hoisted me up.

I gasped. "Ufff."

"You okay?" He loosened his grip.

"Yeah, I just wanted to add some sound effects." I brushed a thumb across his hand. "Thanks for the help." Elated with a mixture of emotions, I couldn't stop grinning.

He reached into the back of the truck bed and handed me a can. "Sorry, I don't have a straw."

"Funny, man." I watched his smile brighten as he flashed lots of teeth, and crinkle lines appeared around his eyes.

Effortlessly, he hiked himself onto the temporary chair.

I sat close enough to feel the heat from his thigh as I stared at the river. Sitting beside Ty as the sky turned into a blaze of orange, yellow, and red was where I wanted to be. A feeling of contentment washed over me. "Wow. What a magnificent sunset."

Ty slid an arm across my shoulders. "Gorgeous."

I rested my weight against him. "This is amazing. I'm so happy. A full belly and beautiful view." I clamped my lips tight before I blurted something I'd later regret.

"Come on. In a few seconds, the mosquitoes will swarm, and I didn't bring bug spray." He jumped from the tailgate, clasped his hands around my waist, and lifted me down.

Resting my hands on his shoulders, I inhaled his fresh scent, wishing we didn't have to go. "Hmmm, once again, thank you for the help, dinner, and being reasonable." I staggered back, hoping the cool night air would temper my desire. The thought of him rebuffing my advances slid the smile from my face. "Hey, are things going any better with you and Travis? Last weekend, you looked like you wanted to punch him."

"Most days, I still do. He comes by in the evenings to help and complain about his ex-wife and new girlfriend. It's hard to hold a grudge against someone so unhappy. The plus side is Trevor is a lot of fun."

"I'm glad you're getting a chance to bond. I always liked Trevor."

"Yeah, he's a goofball, but I like him." He shifted, glanced at the ground, and kicked at a tuft of grass. "Besides, your mom constantly points out this is what Dad wanted. Time for us boys to be together. I feel guilty not coming earlier to help Dad fix the house. But I know he's happy I'm here now, because I keep finding dimes."

I heard the barely audible sound of a buzz and then watched the hungry little bugger land on his forehead. After a sound slap, the only evidence that remained was a splotch of blood above the right eyebrow.

"Hurry." He tossed the beers into the trash.

I scrambled inside.

A moment later, he crawled inside and started the truck but didn't start driving. He gripped the wheel and kept his gaze peering out into the darkness. "It's been a tough week. No matter how hard I worked, thoughts of you popped into my head."

Smiling, I glanced over and brushed his forearm. "Really?"

"I'm not sure if you're surprised or fishing for compliments. But you are a beautiful, smart, funny woman. I'm not sure why you swore off men, but I'm glad you're reconsidering. But..." He flashed a sideways glance before returning his attention to the road. "I can't promise anything. I'm processing a lot right now."

Air whistled between my lips. "I can relate. It's been two years since JR shredded my world with sweet words and promises of a rosy future. But I've never felt comfortable with a one-night stand. I always opted for the works, like romance, promises, and a broken heart. Can people change?"

"They can try." He chuckled.

"But until then, the focus must be on making Mom's spare bedroom habitable. Being here makes me vulnerable. I'm the person who goes to the animal shelter and donates bedding but never makes eye contact with the dogs."

"Why?"

I folded myself into the seat, fanning my face. "I'm worried I'll make a mistake and feel sorry for the first dog that looks my way. Even if I know the dog is a terrible fit, I'd take him home and then regret it." At the sound of his throat clearing, I glanced over and shook my head. "I'm not implying you're the wrong dog." I pushed the hair from my damp face and sighed. "It's just—"

"I get it, but I can't say I won't look at you and imagine our one memorable night."

"And I can't promise I won't kiss you and regret my decision."

He shifted into gear and drove through the park.

With him focused on the road, I stared out the window at the fading scenery. Would one night change things? I exhaled and leaned back. The river road was dark with no traffic, yet I noticed Ty checking his mirrors, both hands on the wheel with white knuckles. Was he looking for someone? Or overly cautious? "Is everything okay?"

"Why?"

"You seem tense."

He switched on the radio, and "I Want To Know What Love Is" by Foreigner drifted from the speakers.

"Just being tactically aware. Carryover from the military." He expanded his chest and blew out a long, slow breath. "Let me know if you spot an IED."

"What?"

His laughter filled the cab. "Just trying to lighten the mood."

Watching him try to adjust to being a civilian made me want to restart my life. The chorus from the Foreigner song repeated in my mind. I picked a piece of dry plaster from my T-shirt. One memorable night.

On the drive back, I stole glances like a teenager instead of being middle-aged. The butterflies and uncertainty also felt like the musing of a much younger me. The sun might have set, but the campers were just getting started. Campfires burned, music blared, and people walked everywhere. I gripped the seat and held my breath until the truck stopped under the trailer. Inhaling, I gasped. "How you do that."

He winked. "Tactical awareness."

Outside the trailer, I smelt the burning logs and the damp riverbank. Voices blended with the music and created a unique sound.

"Want a fire?"

I shook my head. "I'm kind of tired." Lifting my foot onto the bottom step of the trailer, I moaned.

"Yeah, I imagine." He reached around me and unlocked the door.

I struggled up the three stairs and winced as I tried to remove my shoes.

Ty kneaded the muscles around my neck. "Want a back rub?"

"Everyone knows that is code for sex." I softened my gaze.

"Want a massage?"

Gazing into his blue eyes, I wondered why I didn't accept his offer. He wasn't a random stranger. I liked Ty and felt a connection. I winked and watched a slow smile crease his cheeks as he lowered both eyebrows. "Ask me after a shower." I stepped away, gathered my things, and jumped into the tepid shower. I shampooed my hair and skipped the conditioner. Suddenly, I no longer wanted to play the victim. JR had taken so much already, and now I would control the shots. One night. No lies or promises other than memorable.

Stepping from the bathroom, I rushed to the bed. No naked Ty. Was he waiting in the other bedroom? Wearing nothing but a bath towel, I descended the two steps and spotted him fully clothed in the recliner with closed eyes. After calling his name and getting no response, I retraced my steps and slid between the sheets, disappointed.

Sun shone through the window, and the aroma of steamy coffee drifted into the bedroom. I tossed off the covers and rushed down the steps in an oversized T-shirt.

Ty sat in the tiny booth with an empty cup in front of him. He glanced away from his phone. "Good morning." He pointed toward the counter. "Help yourself."

"Thanks." I pulled a pod from the basket. "Want another cup? Or breakfast?" I watched the water trickle and sputter into my cup.

"I already ate. There is a breakfast sandwich on the stove for you."

"Thanks." I brought my food and coffee over to the table. "It's not even eight o'clock."

He swiped a thumb across the phone screen. "Eat up. You have work to do before you head back out of town."

The rich aroma of hazelnut wafted from the steamy mug. Hugging the warm cup, I took an initial sip and peered at him. He didn't seem like the social media type. "What are you reading?"

"Current events."

I picked up and bit through the toasted bun, tasting

the seasoned sausage, creamy egg, and melted cheddar cheese. Was it hunger, or perhaps a secret spice or sauce that made me think this was delicious? With a mouthful of my sandwich, I nodded. "This is good."

"You said the same thing last Sunday."

"I might have to get a sack to take home. I can work until three, and then I need to drive back." After eating and enjoying a second cup of coffee, I gathered my dishes and bumped into Ty.

Standing chest to chest, sandwiched between the island and the stove, he cleared his throat. "A lot of things were said last night. I don't have a woman in every state. In fact, there is no one. But—"

"I know you're only interested in a hooking up, booty call—"

"Stop." He scrubbed a hand across his face. "It's not what I meant. I like you, but with or without the bike, I'm leaving on the first of September and don't plan to return."

"Two years ago, I didn't worry about money. My calendar was full of social events, and after one phone call, everything was gone." I rocked back on my heels, surprised by the sudden emotion. Blinking back a tear, I took a deep breath. "Plans don't work, people die, and things change. I never thought I'd kiss a guy again and see how that turned out."

"A little dramatic." He trailed a finger across my cheek. "I'm sorry you were treated poorly, and he broke your heart."

"Crazy thing is, when I placed the anonymous tip, I was suspended between guilt and relief. I knew the company might shut down and people could lose their jobs. Yet, a small part of me was also happy and gave me a reason to end things with JR. For years, everyone told me how lucky I was to be dating him and how I'd be a fool to let him go, but—"

"The wrong dog." He lowered his head, brushing light, teasing kisses across my cheeks and lips.

I stood motionless.

He ran his hands up and down my back.

The passion ignited, burning away conscious thoughts. I pulled him close, deepening the kiss and going weak at the knees.

He tensed, his lips stilled, and the contact was broken.

Apprehension straightened my muscles. Standing tall, I searched his eyes for an explanation. As the pounding of my pulse weakened, I heard a phone vibrating across the table.

He cocked his head toward the sound.

"Do you need to get that?"

"It could be an emergency." He rushed to grab the phone from the shiny tabletop. "Hey, Travis, what's up?"

I watched as his gaze glanced from me to the window outside. He murmured a lot and seemed hesitant until a smile slid across his lips. "Of course." He disconnected and moved closer. "Seems Travis desperately needs my help."

"You seemed pleased by this development." *Why* lingered on the tip of my tongue. Was this more about getting distance from me or rebuilding a connection with siblings? I could feel my face scrunch. Was it all about the chase for him?

"Come here." But this time, instead of a sweet lingering of lips, he deepened the kiss.

"Oh, Sal."

Breathless, I clutched his shirt.

He leaned back.

Cool air replaced the heat of his mouth. I blinked and tried to bring him back.

"Sal, I've got to go help Travis."

"Why did you kiss me like that if you're leaving?"

"A subtle hint of what you missed. You could have woken me up." He nodded toward the door. "You need to get ready. I told him I could be there in thirty minutes."

On the ride to Mom's house, I opened my mouth a dozen times, wanting to ask if his sudden desire to help had anything to do with needing space. But I couldn't get the words to come out. Standing beside my car, I watched him place the backpack in the backseat before he turned and waved. *What the fudge. No kiss, no hug, just a platonic flapping of his hand.* Confused, I stomped into Mom's house and explained the situation. At the sight of her sneer turning into a smile, I cringed.

"What did you say to have him dump you on my doorstep? Not that I'm complaining."

I started toward the kitchen. "Coffee."

She grasped my arm. "Let's go out. I could use a change of scenery."

Was she lonely without Bernie? "Sure. Do you want to change first?"

She glanced down at the red, orange, and blue skin-tight leggings before tugging on the hem of her black T-shirt. "Just need lipstick. You could probably use some, too."

"Nope, I like the natural look."

"Suit yourself, but besides honey, a little color

always helps attract a mate. Take a lesson from the animals." She hustled down the hall to the bathroom and returned a few minutes later with bright-red lips, six-inch gold hoop earrings, a white shell necklace, and clunky white tennis shoes.

I guess the days of stiletto sandals have passed.

On the drive to Wake and Bakery, she chatted nonstop.

But I didn't respond until she mentioned the bingo pot on Tuesday was over five hundred dollars. "That's a lot of money. I could use that money for the motorcycle classes." I took a sharp right into what looked more like a vacant housing lot. Thinking about what I'd do with cash, I crept toward two older gentlemen who looked like hippies with faded jeans, sandals, and Grateful Dead T-shirts. They sat on one of the felled telephone poles marking the edge of the lot. I inched forward.

"Don't hit the guy with the white beard. He's kind of cute."

"Can you play a bingo card for me?"

"Hey! Whoa!"

Turning toward Mom, I felt the front tires of my car bump into the pole. I slammed the brakes and gasped as the large wooden log slowly rolled back and flipped the men onto their backs.

With their legs extended to the sky, their sandals flapped in the air.

Mom dashed out the door.

I shifted into Park and rushed after her.

Bubbling laughter rose from the men.

Heat scorched my cheeks.

Mom extended a hand and had both men standing.

"I'm so sorry." I gushed. "Are you okay?"

Still laughing, they brushed the dust from their butts.

Mom helped the bearded man get every speck of dirt off his denim pants.

"Should I call paramedics?" I glanced around, hoping no one filmed the incident. The last thing I needed was my face plastered on the media. Only this time, instead of dating a thief, fame would come from rolling two old guys. After assurances from the gentlemen that they were fine, I entered the coffee shop, surprised Mom had followed. The place had a sixties vibe, lively colored beads, tapestries, incense, and music.

"Don't order anything with THC unless you want to call a cab," she whispered.

Fifteen minutes later, I stepped outside with an iced chai latte.

Mom walked beside me, waving a cup piled high with whipped cream.

I sat at the yellow picnic table adjacent to the empty telephone pole. The sun was directly overhead, and the cold tea tasted spicy, sweet, and refreshing.

"Oh, look." She plucked an object from the dirt. "A dime. Someone in heaven is thinking of us." She slid onto the bench seat. "Bernie was probably worried about how many people you'd hit with the bike. Or maybe your daddy is trying to communicate. I think he's saying quit that dead-end job?"

Tilting my face to the sky, I peered at the cloudless day. "Dad, I'm only working because I need health insurance and a steady paycheck."

"Scared, huh?"

I tensed and swallowed a slew of platitudes. I was

tired of lying. "Yeah, I am."

Reaching across the table, she patted my hand. "Me, too. Been that way ever since your daddy died."

I swirled the melted cubes in my cup and took the last sip, lost in thought.

She stood, wiped a smidge of whipped cream from the tip of her nose, and winked. "I'm getting a brownie to go. Should I get two?"

"None for me. The company does random drug tests."

"Another reason to quit that job and enjoy life before it's too late."

"I'll think about it." I sucked in my bottom lip. *Could I change? Where do I start, hair color, tattoo, or a body piercing?*

Chapter Seven

Monday morning was a struggle to get out of bed. Saturday, I must have lifted something wrong because pain seized my back and butt. But I still managed to arrive on time for work. I slipped from my front seat and spotted Joe standing beside a new white sports car. *Did he win the lottery?* I tensed. *Is he embezzling funds?*

I marched over, hand on my hips. "How much do accountants make?"

"More than you. I heard they're posting Wendy's job. You should apply."

"No formal education. Besides, I need to focus on obtaining a motorcycle endorsement. Wait." I pulled my hands off my waist. "Don't sidetrack the conversation. You're driving an expensive new vehicle."

"Yeah, so I got a loan. Oh." He nodded. "Stop worrying. The only fraudulent act here is the interest they charge."

"Sorry, it's just you never mentioned you were looking—"

"Long story short, I wasn't, but this weekend at the dealership, my car fell off the lift. As I'm furiously stomping around the lot, a butterfly lands on my arm." He waved three fingers. "I swear, it's the truth, and I took it as a sign."

"Unbelievable." At the building, a groan whistled through my lips as I reached for the door.

"Let me." He brushed my hand aside. "From how you're moving, I'd guess you did something more than kissing."

"I did a lot more...tore down walls, sheetrock, and hauled junk to a dumpster."

"Seriously, Sal, you need to get a life." He pulled his eyelids together and narrowed his gaze as if he were trying to blot me from his vision.

"It might be better this way."

Joe shook his head. "Staying at a go-nowhere job, moping around your apartment, and struggling to pay bills."

"Damn JR. I should be looking forward to retirement instead of cursing Mondays." I tossed my sandwich onto the third shelf.

"Are you worried Ty will be another JR and screw your mom out of her inheritance, or take your motorcycle?"

Tension stiffened my already tight muscles. "I hadn't even thought of that." Having no desire to continue the conversation, I rushed to my workstation. *Should I trust Ty?* As I waited for the phones to ring, I replayed all my conversations with Bernie's sons and texted Mom.

—*Do you trust Travis, Trevor, and Ty?*—

—*Yep. They're good boys.*—

I returned my attention to the screen. The morning dragged by.

A few minutes before lunch, Mom sent a selfie eating her brownie with the caption—*you don't know what you're missing.*

In the break room, I spotted Lisa and Joe sitting at the table and walked over to share Mom's photo. "She assures me her inheritance is safe as she eats a treat from Wake and Bakery."

"What have I missed?" Lisa gasped.

"Joe greeted me this morning with his latest theory. Ty's another JR. But they're not alike. JR used grand gestures, expensive gifts, romance, and words of love. Whereas Ty constantly tells me he wants the bike, a memorable night, and then he is gone."

"Oh." Lisa grinned. "Do you think if you sleep with him, he'll change his plans?"

"Believe me, I'd never try changing a man's mind." I clenched my hands into fists. Why did I feel agitated? And why was I standing?

"Sounds like the perfect guy." Joe shrugged. "You don't want a relationship."

"I also shy away from going inside the animal shelter because I fear taking a dog home. I meet the volunteers in the parking lot and hand over the kennel blankets and toys."

"Sit." Joe brushed past me, retrieving our lunches from the refrigerator. "You're making absolutely no sense. Why don't you get a pet?"

"How do I choose which dog gets freedom? What if I pick a mean one or he doesn't like me?"

"I'd be afraid of the dog eating my furniture and pooping on the floor." Lisa popped the top on her diet soda.

Joe ripped the lid off his plain yogurt. "Choose a well-behaved, loyal, mutt that loves you."

"What if—"

Lisa slammed her cola down. "Enough about dogs.

Let's get back to Ty. He's the real issue. There will always be animals in need of a home. But this could be your last chance at a summer romance."

"On Saturday night, I was this close." I indicated the distance with my right thumb and index finger. "But he fell asleep while I was in the shower. And on Sunday, he dropped me off at Mom's without a kiss. What kind of guy does—?"

"Not someone who wants to get—"

"Joe!" Lisa twisted in her chair and shushed him.

"Now, I don't know what to do? Should I have a memorable night or keep him in the friend zone?"

"Okay, this should make the decision easier." Lisa sighed. "Imagine yourself in a nursing home, sitting in bed, and waiting for an aid to bring you to the bathroom. Ask yourself if you'd regretted having a summer fling?"

With a swig of stale, tepid coffee, I swallowed the last bite of my peanut butter sandwich. "Maybe? But I'm for sure having second thoughts about whatever I did to get me into the nursing home. What's your regret?"

"Not having one of those cute male nurses snuggled beside me." Lisa laughed.

"You don't even have to look that far away." Joe shook his head. "Think about a year from now. We're sitting at the same table. Your mom is in an apartment with a new man, and you are back at home, sewing. Any regrets?"

The question slammed into my gut like a bowling ball. I sucked in air as a wave of despair washed over me. "Got to get back." Rushing from the room, I blinked away a tear. *What's wrong with me?* I had no regrets about leaving JR and could easily imagine the rest of my nights filled with sewing. *Is it Ty, hormones, or not enough sleep?*

For the next few days, Joe's words haunted me. On Thursday night, I crawled into bed. I didn't want Ty to be my regret.

On Friday, before the alarm sounded, I slipped into the kitchen. As the sun broke the horizon, I sipped coffee in a faded, frayed nightshirt. Why didn't Ty kiss me goodbye on Sunday? Why hasn't he texted? I set the cup next to the quilted heart, picked up my phone, and looked through the texts from Mom to find the screenshot of the message about safety equipment. His phone number appeared at the top of the image.

—Last Sunday, at my mom's, why didn't you kiss me goodbye?—

The phone rang.

I answered after one ring with a shaky hand. "Hello."

"Sal? Good morning. I've been waiting for you to call or text. Your mom wouldn't give me your number, and I never want to kiss you goodbye—"

"Sorry to bother you."

"Let me finish. I'd rather kiss you goodnight."

"Oh." I took a deep breath. Luckily, this was an audible call, and he couldn't see my bewilderment. I already had a lifetime of regrets, but with Ty, I didn't know whether the pain and angst would come from saying *yes or no.*

"No pressure. You need to do what's best for you. But I didn't have time to work on the spare bedroom. So, it's my trailer or your mom's bed?"

Threading my fingers through my hair, I swayed to

an internal beat as the sun drenched my kitchen. *I have a million things to do, pack, pluck, and shave. Do I have time to paint my toes?*

"So?"

"This is the easiest decision I've made. The trailer."

"Great. See you tonight. I'll make dinner."

After a lengthy shower and grooming, I searched through my wardrobe. Most of the clothes still had tags—back when money wasn't a problem, and my happiness came from making purchases. Shaking my head, I looked at the outfits I had no desire to wear. *Guess I can change.* After grabbing a sundress and sweater, denim shorts, jeans, and two shirts, I paused at bedtime attire. Last weekend, I had worn an oversized T-shirt, but if Ty offered a back rub, I wanted to look good. I found last year's Christmas gift of sleepwear from Wendy still in the box. Cherry mini-shortie bottom with whipped scallop edging and matching spaghetti-strapped tank out of the softest cotton. I pulled them out, and a note fluttered to the ground.

It's more fun to give than receive. Go give someone a thrill by wearing these to bed.

Not one to talk to the dead, I did mouth *thank you.* She would have enjoyed the latest development in my life and encouraged me to enjoy the weekend. I placed everything on the bed, slipped into clean yoga pants, and pulled a tunic top over my head before making a hasty lunch and going out the door. At work, I couldn't stop checking the clock or smiling.

By lunchtime, Lisa broke my resolve with her spidery sense for romance.

I told her about the early morning call.

"Glad to hear you're taking my advice." Joe nudged me with his elbow.

Lisa slapped his arm. "I'm the one who said to give Ty a chance."

Even though I stated no decision had been made, the desired outcome was obvious. At home, I packed everything I had preselected and stacked on the bed in a backpack before taking a quick shower. Afterwards, I twirled in front of the mirror in a pop floral sleeveless dress of pink, white, teal-blue, and navy. I added a few sprays of my favorite fragrance, a floral scent with a citrus undertone. Would Ty's bedroom smell like a fruit salad in the morning?

****

Three hours later, I parked next to Ty's blue truck.

He rushed over dressed in brown fitted shorts and a cream-colored long sleeve T-shirt. "Hey, Beautiful." He held open the driver's door.

"Hey." I dried my palms on the car seat before standing.

He wrapped both arms around me and hip-checked the door closed. "You smell good." With bright-blue eyes, he lowered his lips for a quick kiss. "I like the dress."

Tangling my fingers into the short hairs at the nape of his neck, I pulled him closer. "You smell like summer, sunscreen, and campfires."

A deep rumble of laughter shook his body and mine. He brushed another kiss across my lips. "Hungry? I made a salad, and the steaks are ready to grill."

On steadier legs, I stepped back. "What do you need me to help with?"

"Can you open the wine?"

"Besides cooking and washing dishes, I'm skilled at pulling a cork."

He twirled me and dipped me low for another kiss. "An accomplished woman of many talents."

Heat moved from the tips of my toes to the top of my head. The sudden need, wanting, and pounding heart made me feel alive and womanly.

Adjacent to his camper, a red-and-white-checked tablecloth covered the picnic table, and a mason jar with white and pink mini roses served as a centerpiece. The place setting for two and the bottle of wine added to the romantic scene.

He shifted and ran a hand over the top of his head.

Is he nervous, too? "Everything looks great. I love the flowers. Wow, you didn't have to go to so much trouble."

Grinning, he swooped down and placed a slight kiss on my cheek. "No problem. I'll run in and get the rest of the stuff."

"Need help?"

"I got it. Just relax."

Leaning over the table, I brushed a thumb across the soft petals of the flowers. Something about him taking the time to create an intimate setting magnified the consequences of getting involved. What if the expectations of the evening fell flat? Everything would be awkward. Could we still be friends? I shifted my gaze from the wheels on the camper to his truck, and if things turned out great…what was the point when everything was temporary?

Taking a deep breath, I vowed to stay in the moment and not worry about the end of summer. A love song from the seventies floated from the outdoor speakers. And with the sun dipping lower in the sky, I wasn't slapping my arms or legs. He must have sprayed for insects, or the smoke from distant campfires or the citronella candles persuaded the mosquitoes to feast elsewhere.

The trailer door opened, and he reappeared, placing the steaks on the grill.

The sound of meat sizzling filled the air with a tantalizing and slightly smoky smell. I could feel a rumble in my stomach. "How was your week?"

He sprinkled seasonings onto the steaks. "I got very little done at the house. Travis' project turned out to be a bigger job than either of us expected. Someone offered him free vinyl fencing, and his girlfriend thought they…" He emphasized the word with air quotes. "Meaning mostly me should enclose the backyard for her yappy ankle biters.

I softened my gaze and marveled at how freely he gave his service to others. "Did you finish the project?"

"Yep, on Thursday." His grin widened and created wrinkles around his eyes. "And on Friday morning, the dogs were running around the neighborhood. They dug under the fence for freedom. I'm thinking of blocking Travis' number."

"Such brotherly love."

He flipped the steaks. The meat sputtered as the flames briefly flared up. "They're a pain, but I'm glad I have them, and it's been fun working together."

"Never thought I'd hear those words."

"Surprised me, too."

I told him about Joe and Lisa and how I spent the day scheduling service technicians for repairs and sales

95

personnel for quotes on new heating and cooling equipment.

"Do you enjoy your job?" He held my gaze.

Is he curious or judging? I shrugged. "Often I'm bored, but it's a steady paycheck, and I have health insurance. Before JR came to work for his father, I loved working at the construction firm." I sighed, not wanting to go there. "You must have liked your job in the military."

He placed the cooked steaks on plates, set them on the picnic table, and dumped a bag of salad mix into a bowl. "There are plusses and minuses to a military career. The biggest downsides were deployments, which made relationships difficult."

I uncorked the bottle of pinot noir from Oregon. "Smells good, fruity with hints of blackberries, and cherries."

"A buddy of mine suggested the wine. I thought if it's good, I might go visit."

Pushing away thoughts of the future, I focused on the moment, poured two glasses, and gave him one. "To new friendships and summer." After tapping glasses, I paused and waited for him to take a sip.

"To an amazing woman." He held my gaze.

For two years, I thought of myself as the felon's fiancée and now to hear him calling me amazing… I wanted to throw my arms around him, hold on, and never let go. "Thank you."

Ten minutes later, seated at the table, I stabbed the caramelized steak and cut off a small piece. "*Mmm.* Savory and slightly smokey." I nodded my approval. "For someone who can't cook, this is delicious."

"Burgers, hotdogs, and bag opening are the extent

of my culinary skills."

"I'm not complaining. I see nothing wrong with salad and protein. What about chicken?"

With a pinched mouth, he shook his head. "If you like it dry and chewy."

"I'll cook the poultry…"

For the rest of the meal, the conversation evolved around favorite foods, movies, and music. The casual exchange of ideas tugged at distant memories and the dream of companionship. Someone to ask about my day…to sit across the table and gaze into their eyes instead of staring at social media scrolls.

After dinner, I welcomed the warmth of his hand as I walked beside him to the river's edge. The sun dipped beneath the horizon, bathing the campground in hues of red, orange, and yellow. As the sky grew darker, I couldn't keep my apprehension from growing.

Ty wrapped an arm around me. "Cold?"

"Kind of."

On our walk back, I listened to fires crackling, hushed voices, and singing crickets. The steps outside the trailer creaked as I climbed inside. Lights glowed in the kitchen as I turned on the water to wash the dishes.

He bumped into me. "Thanks, although you—"

"I don't mind washing. You can dry." With every touch, excitement, anticipation, and second thoughts bubbled up inside me like a shaken can of soda.

Ty took a dripping plate from my hands and began drying. "I asked my dad why he didn't marry your mom, and he said she turned him down. Something about your father dying in the war and her getting widow's benefits."

"During the Vietnam Conflict, my dad lost his life.

Since then, Mom has rejected all proposals. She claims it's the pension, but maybe she never wanted to be anyone else's wife."

"Did you ever ask her?"

I rolled my eyes. "Of course, what girl isn't interested in who her dad was and why she didn't have a stepfather? Occasionally, she told me about my daddy. What he looked like in high school, his favorite foods, and how he made her feel like a princess. Then her eyes would mist up, and she started hollering about wasting time when things needed to be done. So, I learned to ask my grandma. She told me lots of stories. They had been high school sweethearts, and before he left for Vietnam, they were married at a courthouse ceremony. He died without even knowing he'd be a father. His parents never acknowledged the wedding or me." Pulling the stopper from the sink, I watched the water swirl before disappearing down the drain and heard a plate rattle against the counter.

"I'm so sorry."

Blinking back the sudden tears, I dried my hands. Being a soldier, Ty understood things better than most. "Sometimes, I think she believes life did her an injustice. She wanted a rebel daughter, who'd shake her fist at injustice, and fix a broken world. But she got me."

"Nothing wrong with you. Your mom is tough to figure. When I showed up this morning, I expected to be jabbed with an ice cream cone for disappearing all week, but instead of complaining, she tried to take me to breakfast." He brushed a thumb across my cheek.

"It wasn't the Wake and Bakery, was it?"

"You make life interesting. I know I've been

moody. It's a transition being with civilians." He shifted and dimmed the lights. The soft beat of a classic love song pulsed from the surround sound system. "Found any hearts or dimes?"

Slipping my fingers through the belt loops of his jeans, I pulled him closer. "No. Have you?"

"This morning, after you texted, a dime appeared in the gravel behind the camper." He looped his arms around my waist and started dancing.

Raising my left eyebrow, I searched his face for a hint of a smile and found none. "Do you think your dad is thinking about you? Or do you believe the coin was a coincidence?"

He hummed along to half the song before pausing. "After being deployed, I know there are things that have no explanation. When I picked up the coin, for a moment, I felt at peace."

The warmth from his body and the glass of wine put me in a happy place. I followed the lead of my mystery man, swaying in the small space between the reclining loveseats and the entertainment center.

"Sal, you don't have to decide anything this weekend. I can see the questions and hesitation in your eyes. From what I have heard, JR was a con man, but not everyone is a cheat and a liar."

"I know you're not him, but what if—"

He dipped me low and brought me back. "Today, a country song played on the radio. The girl fears getting played, but...what if the relationship turns out great?"

" "What If" by Kane Brown and Lauren Alaina."

"Yeah, that's the one." He tilted his right hip before shifting to the left in slow, rhythmic movements. "What if…"

I swallowed down the words. *But you are leaving and this is temporary.* "What were you like in high school? A jock, a nerd, or a ladies' man?" I blurted the first question that came to mind, stopping the thought of goodbye at the end of summer.

"Amber."

I stepped on his toes.

"Ouch!"

"I figured you had a history."

"Yep, Dad told me to stay clear of her. Called her my BIF?"

"Huh?" I clung to him, inhaling his scent, as I no longer followed the beat of the song but merely swayed.

"Bad-influence friend. Of course, being seventeen, I did the total opposite. She was twenty-one and could buy liquor. Senior year, my grades failed. I got kicked off the football team and lost my scholarship. At nineteen, the cops pulled me over for reckless driving. The judge gave me the choice of jail or the armed service. The best thing that ever happened." Ty spun me out of his arms and then back again.

Swaying, I held him tight.

"But what if…" He tangled his fingers in my hair, placing kisses across my cheeks.

"About that back rub." I danced with him to the stairs leading to the bedroom, eager to slip into the silky nightwear and wondering how long he'd let me stay in my sleepwear?

****

With the sun shining through the blinds, I heard noises and hoped he was defrosting breakfast sandwiches. But instead of rushing, I stretched, remembering his touches. How could anything that felt so right be a wrong choice? I tugged the cherry tank top over my head and went to find coffee.

Ty stood next to the kitchen table, dressed in jeans and a teal T-shirt. His gaze traveled over my body. "Morning, Beautiful. Unfortunately, your mom has club members coming over to do wiring and plumbing today."

Standing on the bottom step, I shifted my smile to a pout. If I were confident, I'd sashay across the floor, wrap my arms around him, and ask him to take the morning off. I stepped down. *What if he laughs at my request? Demands I get dressed?* Heat stung my cheeks as I stood on the cold tile floor. I turned toward the stairs. "Give me fifteen minutes, and can you make me a coffee?"

"Ten, and you can have one of my famous breakfast sandwiches."

I stood under semi-warm water for under two minutes before wrapping a towel around my body. Shivers rushed from my toes to my head as fragments of the evening flashed.

"Sal, hurry if you want coffee."

After tugging on shorts and a shirt, I stepped lazily into the kitchen, stretched, and tucked the hair behind my ears.

He walked over and brushed kisses against my neck.

Wrapping both arms around him, I held him tight and felt the rapid beat of my heart.

"Hmmm. That's quite a hug." He winked. "The members can manage without us for a few more minutes."

Besides the blood-pounding desire heightening my

physical responses, I enjoyed a flicker of self-assurance. *He likes me and finds me desirable.* I raced back up the stairs with Ty close behind.

****

After making the bed for the second time in the day, I took another quick shower and opted for coffee at the gas station.

Ty purchased a dozen donuts and breakfast sandwiches for the volunteer workers.

Walking in with the food was a great idea. I helped Ty hand out the sandwiches as I introduced myself. Everyone seemed to have a story to share about Bernie. The day flew past. I spent most of the afternoon staying out of the workers' way and scraping wallpaper from the spare bedroom and thinking about Ty. Finally, at three o'clock, the club members left, but not before talking us into volunteering at The Club tonight for the monthly steak dinner.

Ty tugged me into the corner of the kitchen. "I'm cooking steaks. Did they talk you into dishes?"

"Nope, serving meals. At least we'll get home early."

He pulled me close and kissed me until my toes curled.

"Don't mean to interrupt." Mom wedged between us. "But can you give me a ride tonight? They need my help behind the bar."

"Sure." Ty nodded. "Just going to head home to clean up, but can be back around four thirty to pick you up."

Mom smirked. "First, it was submarine races, making out, and now it's called clean up? Whatever. Don't be late."

With the sun still high in the western sky, Ty parked the truck. "Welcome home. I've been thinking about this all day. Want a back rub?"

From the passenger seat, I gestured. "Are you a little stiff?"

Ty slipped out the door. "Last one in gets the lotion?"

After wrestling with my seatbelt, I caught up before his feet hit the stairs. "No fair, you had a head start." The merriment in my voice blended with the squealing kids tearing up and down the dirt road on bikes and scooters.

He fumbled, trying to get the key in the lock. Laughing, he glanced down, stilled, and shifted his eyes to the right.

At his reaction, shivers raced up my spine. The pounding of my pulse increased, then slowed as I recognized Barb. "I didn't hear you walk over."

"I am old, but stealthy. Want to join us for a beer?"

Wayne trailed behind his wife, nodding.

Ty chewed on his bottom lip and shifted his gaze between me and Barb. Did he have difficulty with saying *no*? Was he thinking of all the times he missed with his dad? I exhaled. "Sure. Although only one, Ty promised Mom a ride to The Club." I watched Ty smile and knew having a beer was the right decision. Something about making him happy pleased me. How would I ever say goodbye at the end of the summer?

****

After dropping off Mom, the sun was setting when Ty backed the truck under the front cap of the fifth wheel.

I climbed from the truck and strained to hear the

voices and music of the other campers. With darkness, a reverent hush had fallen over the campground, and I felt like I was in church. Only a few campfires twinkled in the distance.

Ty looped an arm around my waist. "Want to take a walk?"

"It's so dark."

"The moon must be behind a cloud. But don't worry, your eyes will adjust. At the end of the island, the stars are the brightest."

Strolling over the dirt road together, I inhaled the lingering smells of grilled meats, the river, and campfire smoke. Couples waved and occasionally called out a greeting. The only people not outside were those in big rigs whose TVs glowed through large glass windows.

The path narrowed, snaking through an outcrop of trees before opening to a large grass area. "If I had a camper, this is the spot I'd want to park."

"According to Wayne, this end of the island floods, and after getting tractors to drag out the sunken RVs, they changed this to a tent-only section." He draped an arm over my shoulder and directed me to the water's edge.

The few clouds trailed south, exposing a full moon that cast a silver glow to the ripples lapping against the shore. The bank to the east was nothing more than black shadows, and downriver, the lights from a barge or tug boat twinkled.

Ty pointed out the Big Dipper, North Star, and Orion's Belt as I mentally counted the weekends until the end of summer. *Eight.*

"Everything okay?"

"Just thinking about how much I'll miss…" I waved my arms to encompass all I could see and swallowed the words, *our time together.*

"Look!" He pointed to a star shooting through the sky. "Make a wish."

I closed my eyes. *Before summer ends, may our hearts be in sync.*

As the river rushed past, a lustrous silver-gray moon rode higher above the horizon.

Looking into his eyes, I saw longing and felt the quickening of my pulse. I parted my lips.

He lowered his mouth with a kiss as gentle as a whisper.

Face to face and soul to soul, I could feel time slowing as my focus shifted from the outside world to me. The waves no longer washed against the beach. The sounds of distant traffic and music faded. Passion, want, and desire drew me closer like a magnet to steel. He claimed my heart. As the kiss ended, I followed his lead and waltzed from the bank of the river to the grassy field. With a light touch, I spun, looping under his arms before returning to his embrace.

When our feet stopped, he leaned closer. "Ready to see if wishes come true?"

The warmth of his words echoed in my thoughts. Walking back, I knew I'd never regret one moment spent with him.

****

Early Sunday morning, I helped Ty carry in boxes of donuts for the crew helping at Mom's house.

By one, the workers had completed the plumbing and electrical jobs except for fixtures and switch plates. After a late lunch, the club members headed home.

Mom and the brothers planned on listing the house for sale on the first of August. If everything went according to plan, the prospective buyer would take possession in September.

I joined Ty and Trevor downstairs, tossing junk. The first to go were hundreds of yogurt, margarine, and plastic cottage cheese containers. Next were boxes of musty clothes, newspapers, and magazines. "Why?" I shrugged.

Ty held up a coffee can. "Bent, rusted nails. I never want to own a home."

After a dozen trips, I stopped in the kitchen, sat, and swiped the moisture from my brow.

Mom stepped over to the table and glared.

"What? Did I smear dirt across my forehead?"

"Don't play with me. You've been rushing all weekend." Mom placed her hands on her hips and leaned into my space. "What happened to the plan?"

The sound of basement stairs creaking and boisterous laughter stopped Mom from continuing her interrogation.

A moment later, Travis joined Ty and Trevor standing around the open refrigerator.

Travis pushed the damp curls from his forehead. "Had to be a hundred degrees in the garage, but at least, most of the junk is out. Get me one of those beers."

Trevor pulled out a couple of cans. "Anyone else want one?"

"Go ahead. I was just telling Sal. You boys are working too hard. Ty, take a few weeks off." Mom directed her gaze at me and nodded. "Everyone should enjoy a bit of summer. You should go up and visit Sal in the cities. They have great restaurants. You could go to a concert. He should come see you for a change."

"Actually, I don't mind driving. There isn't much in the city to do in the summer. Minneapolis is more of a spring and fall type of place."

Mom grabbed my chin and tilted my neck. "Did something fall on your head, Sal? The city is the best in the summer."

I pushed her hand away as I scooted back a few feet. Images of all the places we could go flashed like the credits at the end of a movie. Walking with his hand in mine around the Sculpture Garden, lakes, the zoo, and—the ideas abruptly halted. Would he remember me stating I lived in a one-bedroom? Uncertainty clenched my stomach. If I had taken Mom in, then they could have listed the house, but he would have missed out on spending time with his brothers and me.

"If Sal wants to issue an invite, that's her call." Ty shrugged. "But I'd rather get this house listed and be on my way. Even if the campground didn't close after the first hard freeze, I don't want to live in Wisconsin when winter comes."

The thought of Ty rushing to leave after spending the weekend together felt like being punched in the stomach. I stood, crossed my arms over my chest, and scowled in his direction.

He moved closer to the table, brushed a palm against my forehead, and smoothed my furrowed brows. "I'm in a hurry to list the house, but I'm not in a hurry to say goodbye." He winked.

Resting a hand on his chest, I smiled. "It's almost seven o'clock."

"Mabel, I'm taking Sal to the trailer to get her car. I'll be back on Monday."

"Me, too." Travis brushed the red curls from his eyes. "I've got a load of rock being delivered sometime this week. Might need a little help."

"Let me know." Ty turned toward me and rolled his eyes. At the campground, he stepped from the truck.

Barb and Wayne rushed over.

"Hey, kids." Barb waved. "Do you have jumper cables?"

"Sure do. I'll be over in a couple of minutes." He unlocked the trailer door and ushered me through.

Inside the small kitchen area, he sighed as his right hand slid to my forearm. "Even though it'll be a busy week, if you need a back rub—"

I liked not having to wait a week to see him, but until I told him about the second bedroom, I wasn't issuing an invitation and snuffling out his feelings for me. I sensed he might be warming up to the idea of hanging around a bit longer. "Thanks, but let me see if I can get a day or two off of work."

"Just know, I'd rather kiss you good night." He pulled me tight and gazed into my eyes. "I enjoyed having you here."

Looping my arms over his neck, I stood, cataloging all the details...the blue in his eyes, the stubble on his chin, the way his smile crinkled the corners of his eyes. Did I need to get home?

He lowered his lips to mine and kissed me deeply.

Breathless, I created some space. "You're making leaving difficult."

"That's my plan. Stay the night and head back in the morning. Please."

Spending another night in his arms sounded better than grocery shopping and laundry. But leaving at four in the morning sounded horrible. Besides, I need time to sort through these feelings. "I'd better get on the road." I stepped back. "Just need to go upstairs and get my bag."

He dropped his gaze to the floor and shrugged. "Yeah, I've got jumper cables to deliver."

Outside, I tossed the backpack inside and watched Ty stride across the lawn separating the two trailers. I slipped into the front seat, giving a haphazard wave before closing the door. *Why do I feel like I'm leaving a part of myself behind?*

****

On Monday, I bypassed saying *hello* to Joe, walked into the lunchroom, and poured a cup of coffee.

Joe rushed to my side. "Morning to you, too. You're glowing, and I don't have time to talk. They hired a bulldog to replace Wendy." He tapped his watch.

I stepped from the kitchen with a steamy coffee, a little surprised Joe hadn't followed me back to my desk. The calls and administrative work did not keep me busy. Lisa also must have had time on her hands because she stopped.

"You look ten years younger. Don't tell me you're in love." Lisa leaned closer.

"What?" I widened my gaze. "Ty. Nothing more than something to remember in the nursing home."

"When you say his name, you have a glow. There's a softness in your voice. Nothing is wrong with falling in love. Grandmother told me to fall as often as possible, even if it's with the same man."

I glanced at the phone. *Please ring.*

"Are you going to tell him?"

The mere thought increased my pulse to an erratic level. "No."

Joe appeared from around the corner. "Heads up, the new hire left the building and won't return until Monday. What were you talking about?"

"Doesn't matter?"

Lisa tossed her arms up. "Imagine yourself in the skilled nursing facility, and all you can think about is, what if I had told him? Would he have confessed his love? Maybe he would have stayed, and you'd have more than a summer of memories."

"Why can't I be on a beach? Sitting on a tropical island, holding a fruity drink in a pineapple, with a little paper pink umbrella."

Joe shrugged. "Okay, you're on a beach alone. It's your last sunset. Do you wish you would have told Ty?"

"Hmmm. I'm sitting on a blue-and-white-striped beach towel, flip-flops with giant plastic orange flowers, and the waves lap against the shore. You walk over holding a tray of drinks and offer me another beverage and ask if I have any regrets."

"Well." Joe leaned closer. "Do you?"

"I release my last breath into the world without answering. Now go. I have work to do."

The lights on my phone flashed.

I picked up the phone. "Good afternoon, Smith and Sons."

After a quick wave, they left.

Work dragged on with mild summer temperatures. No one was interested in spending money on updating their air conditioners, so I had no issue taking Friday off. I texted Ty to let him know I'd arrive on Thursday night.

He responded with lots of emojis.

—*Sal, don't tell your mom. Unless, of course, you'd rather spend your time with her.*—

—*Not a word from me. I miss you.*—

After fifteen minutes, I gave up thinking he'd respond. Disappointed he didn't reply with, *I miss you, too. Or can't wait to see you.* I silently fumed until I recalled his words. *I'd rather kiss you good night than goodbye.* The sensation of melting softened my facial features as I wrapped my arms around my waist. *Ty's so sweet.* I swayed gently. *Is this love?*

Chapter Eight

On Thursday night, I pulled into the campground at a little after nine and parked next to Ty's truck. The campsite was bathed in an orange glow from the setting sun. As I gathered my things from the front seat, I watched Ty push out of a chair next to the fire ring with small flames and wisps of rising smoke.

He rushed over and opened the car door.

I slid from the front seat, into his embrace. As the intensity of his hug increased, I flinched. Had something happened? Did one of his brothers get into an accident? Did Mom fall? Had he reconnected with Amber? "Everything okay?"

Without loosening his hold, he whispered, "I expected you around eight."

"Road construction and traffic. Apparently, everyone started the weekend early." I inhaled. *Apple orchard in the fall.*

He swung me around. "I'm so happy to see you. I was worried."

The words made me giddy. I repeated the phrase until I felt the ground. How would I hide my growing feelings? Does he like me more, too? How does a person ask?

"Your choice. Drinks outside by the fire, dinner, bed?"

I shifted my gaze from Ty to the crackling logs.

"After a long drive, with too much traffic, a few minutes to unwind by the fire..." I lowered my voice. "Besides the chatter from the frogs and crickets, everything is peaceful."

He looped an arm over my shoulders. "I'm glad you're here to enjoy this with me." After a few steps, he stopped, tilted my chin with the pad of his thumb, and gazed into my eyes.

The pounding of my heart increased and I knew I had fallen in love with Ty.

I clutched his shirt and raised my lips to his mouth. The chatter in my mind grew quiet as the strength in my legs weakened.

He loosened his grasp and stepped back.

With my fingers still clutching his shirt, I attempted to pull him closer.

He brushed the hair from my face. "If you want wine, you need to stop distracting me. Sit." He lowered his lips to the pulse point below my ear. "I could kiss you all night long."

A shiver shook my body. But for how many more nights would he be here to kiss me? The thought tossed me from the moment like a sneeze.

"Everything okay?" Frown lines creased his forehead as his hands rubbed the outside of my arms.

Should I tell him I had feelings for him and dreaded saying goodbye at the end of summer?

"Summer is short. Don't complicate things with thinking." His jaw clenched.

Pinching the bridge of my nose, I took a shaky breath. *Am I annoyed with Ty or myself?* I brushed past him and plopped into the red canvas hammock chair.

"I'll get the wine."

A shiver shot through me. Clearly, he didn't have feelings, but then why was he worried when I was late? So, maybe… But he's leaving, taking the bike, and my heart with him. *What to do? Stay or leave?* At the sound of the trailer door shutting, I glanced at Ty.

He crept closer, holding stemless glasses of wine that threatened to splash over the rim. He had a crooked grin and eyes the color of a cloudless sky.

I slowly reached for a drink.

"A toast, to perfect summer evenings."

"Let me take a sip first, or I'll end up wearing it." The first taste warmed me with the subtle hints of blackberries and cherries. I raised my glass. "Cheers."

A muted click caused the contents to splash precariously close to the rim.

Not wanting to spill, I drank a little more, and heat radiated from my abdomen. "Nice pairing, not too sweet, blends well with the crisp cool evening, setting sun, and you."

He responded by drinking a healthy portion of the pinot noir and settled into his own chair.

I stared at the flames licking at the logs in the fire ring. Had I overreacted to his comment about thinking? Did I want to ruin the evening worrying about something that might not happen? Everyone constantly harped about living in the moment.

The canvas rustled beside me. "Come here."

Instead of protesting that the chair would crumple under our combined weight, I moved over. Tonight, I'd have no concerns about a tomorrow that might never come.

He set his glass down.

Wedged between him and the fabric I heard the

aluminum frame moan and creak. Cautiously, I shifted my weight, and miraculously, I didn't fall.

"Now, this is the perfect pairing." He picked up his wine.

I snuggled beside him, listening to tales about his childhood, and wondering why he never talked about his deployments.

Every ten minutes, he'd stiffen and scan the surrounding area.

The tension inside of him made me realize he had led a different life. Living in the city, I rarely considered the danger, even though I knew people died and were injured daily. The only crime I had experienced was JR's embezzlement and fraud. With Ty rocking in this hammock chair, his body seemed poised for fight or flight. Did his alertness stem from training, deployments, or did his caution come naturally?

"So, JR?"

I sighed. "How much did Mom blab about my past?"

"Only to mention it's good to see you having fun after the drama."

"The only good thing about JR is I didn't marry him before they hauled him off to jail." I shifted. "You have any skeletons in the closet? Regrets?"

"No." He drew me closer. "I'm lucky. I had the chance to tell Dad I loved him before he passed, and after twenty-plus years in the Army, I'm walking away with all my limbs. Couldn't ask for more than that."

"Joe and Lisa, my co-workers, always talk about your last days on Earth. And looking back, is there someone you wished you would have kissed or told you loved?"

"You get refills, and I'll toss another log onto the fire."

Knowing he didn't plan on answering motivated me to give up the comfort and the heat from his body. On the counter sat a box of red blended wine. Tomorrow, the weekend started, and the evening wouldn't be as enjoyable with the jumble of noise, lights, and smoke. I pulled out the spigot and filled the glasses.

Outside once again, I snuggled into the same chair. Ty's arm rested on my shoulder.

He expelled a long, slow breath. "In junior high, I wished I kissed Molly." He shook his head. "In high school, Amber taught me a lot about drinking, drugs, and pleasing a woman." He grinned. "Definitely regret the back-to-back deployments and my marriage ending."

"So, after your wife, you gave up on relationships, and switched to hooking up, or as you like to say, only one memorable night?"

He laughed, and his body rumbled in the canvas chair.

"I didn't have a nine-to-five job. I couldn't let my sexual involvement exceed my knowledge or commitment to the other person."

Skewing my facial features, I glared. "And now?"

He put our glasses onto the ground, trailing kisses from my earlobe to my lips, as his hand brushed the skin of my abdomen.

The chair rocked and moaned, or did the noise come from me?

"Come on, gorgeous, time for bed."

The swing tittered as the frame creaked and groaned.

Ty reached down and tugged me into a stand. The bit of canvas and metal seemed like an omen or a metaphor. I giggled. By summer's end, the two of us might be a bit worn, but still together.

The magic of the evening followed us inside the trailer. After setting the glasses in the sink, I wrapped both arms around him and leaned against the kitchen island. "I like coming here and enjoy being with you. The campground is different. In the apartment, only a wall separates me from the person next door, and here, there is more distance, yet everything is cozier." I leaned in, and his lips tasted like wine.

He shifted his feet and swayed.

The dance felt familiar, yet different. Pressed against his chest, I clasped my hands behind his neck, feeling the vibrations from our pounding hearts. "I love—"

He tensed, jumping back with arched eyebrows and wide-opened eyes.

"Glamping. I love being in the camper."

"Yeah. Me, too. Can't wait to get on the road and enjoy the freedom the road will offer me."

The buzz from the wine vanished. Was he in a hurry to leave me, River City, or memories of his father?

"Come on. It's late."

"I didn't mean—"

He slipped an arm under my knees.

"What are you doing?" I struggled.

"Sal, if you want me to drop you…"

"I want a lot of things, but broken bones aren't on

the list."

"You've gotten a lot heavier. How much wine did you drink?"

"Too much or not enough. Did you just call me fat?"

"Never. You're perfect." He took a few more steps and set me down.

The hairs on my arms vibrated with excitement, the flutter in my chest increased, my gaze softened, and I parted my lips. *Perfect.* I wrapped my arms around him, plopped into the loveseat, and pulled him with me.

"What's your dream, besides becoming a wrestler and body-slamming unexpected men into furniture?"

"What? Like tonight or a year from now?"

"Where would you like to see yourself in a year?" He slid an arm around me, drawing me into the crook of his elbow. "Answer honestly."

"In a home, with a rescue dog. Do you like animals?"

He brushed a kiss on the top of my head. "Who wouldn't want a loyal companion who loved you no matter what and was always happy to see you? But why a house?"

"All my life, I've had temporary homes. Mom never stayed with any guy for more than a couple of years. The never knowing where I'd put my treasures, books, diary, and jeans." I dropped my shoulders, feeling anxious and sad.

"What kind of dog?"

As I focused on the mental image of my imaginary friend, I smiled. "Medium-sized, a little broken, and in need of love. Scruffy with short hair. Nothing fussy. No high maintenance." I rubbed my hand over the top of his head.

"My dog will like to travel and take long walks." He leaned closer and brushed his lips against mine.

A sweet lingering kiss, like a lazy rainy day where you lay in bed. I curled up in his arms and rested my head on his chest.

That night, instead of the trailer rocking like a washing machine on tilt, we set the camper swaying like a boat bobbing over the waves.

On Saturday evening, Ty and I drove into the campground a little after the dinner hour, but he'd spent most of the day distracting me with kisses instead of sanding the baseboard trim.

His brothers and Mom made a lot of rumbling noises when they happened upon us, but I didn't care.

After the truck stopped under the camper, I raced Ty to the trailer door. Laughing, he fumbled with the lock.

I heard our names and turned.

Barb and Wayne waved their arms. "Kids, come over for some beers."

Ty waved back. "Need to clean up first." Inside the trailer, he wrapped his arms around me. "I've wanted to do this all day." He pulled the shirt over my head.

I yanked the belt from his jeans. And thirty minutes later, I walked with Ty over to the neighbors.

"About time." Wayne clapped his hands. "I've got a treat for you. I purchased a variety of craft beers, and we're having a tasting and a pairing." He waved his hands like a game show host, calling attention to a table with paddles crafted from pallet lumber. Each board held five small glasses.

Wayne held his right hand high.

Ty slapped his palm.

Smiling over their exuberance, I followed Barb into the trailer.

She pulled a few items from the refrigerator and added them to the trays. "I've been waiting all day for you two to come back. I have specialty nuts, crackers, cheese, pretzels, and sauces to pair with the beverages."

Outside, seated around the picnic table with beers and food, I exchange a glance with Ty who grinned and winked. They had little name tents for the beverages and labeled toothpicks for the cheese curds, sausages, and sauces. "You guys have really put in the work. Thank you, and the next dinner will be on us." I nodded toward Ty.

"Yep." Ty picked up a small taster glass of beer. "But instead of cooking, I'll make reservations. To good friends, good food, and summer nights."

Everyone raised a glass of beer, clinking the tiny glass rims.

The first beer was very light and tasted like pilsner. I watched Barb pass around small paper plates labeled. *Bloody-Mary-flavored cheese curds*. I squinted and tentatively stuck a toothpick into a non-uniform-shaped small chunk of yellow cheese with specks of red. "Another first."

"I forgot you are a Minnesota gal. The creamery packages the freshest curds warm and straight from the vat. You'll know it's fresh because you can hear the squeak when you bite into it. You are in for a big treat."

Wayne laughed. "Usually, I like a beer chaser with my drink, not the other way around."

I bit into the springy curd, not expecting to hear anything, but as I pierced the cheese, I heard an audible squeak. The first taste was salty, followed by celery, black pepper, dill, and chili flavors. When the plate came around again, I stabbed a few more curds. With the next beer came a round of little sausages with a creamy horseradish sauce for dipping.

As the evening progressed, the sunset and music blared from the surrounding campgrounds. The songs were a mixture of country, pop, and classic old rock. Outside, party lights twinkled, campfires glowed, golf carts whizzed past, and the occupants beeped and waved.

Ty slipped an arm around my waist and pulled me closer.

"A perfect evening." I raised a garlic cheese curd. "You'll have to give me the name of the creamery."

Barb nodded. "For sure, I hope you kids are coming back next year."

Would there be a next year?

"Nope." Ty shook his head. "So, let's plan for dinner next Saturday. My treat."

Wayne leaned back, tapping his chin. "Barb, honey, wasn't there that fancy steak house downtown you've been dying to try?"

"Oh, Wayne, don't tease. It's our pleasure having you come over."

Ty turned and caught my gaze. He mouthed, *dinner?*

I answered with a smile.

"Fancy steaks." Ty rubbed his hands together. "I'll make the reservations."

Thirty minutes later, the guys put out the campfire. Darkness crept over the area, and the sound of crickets replaced the music.

In the kitchen, I stretched and yawned. "That was fun, and I'm stuffed."

An old Trisha Yearwood song, "Thinkin' About You" drifted softly from the speakers.

Ty drew me close. Humming the melody as he started our bodies in motion, swaying to the music. When the song ended, he closed his eyes and murmured another line.

The sensation of being connected constricted my throat. Blinking, I looked up and whispered, "If this isn't love—"

"Sal, it's not you."

I covered his mouth. "Don't you dare say that!" His shirt bunched beneath the fingers on my left hand as tension vibrated through my muscles like vocal cords. "I didn't profess my undying love, but what's wrong with having feelings? This wasn't something I had planned or chosen. One day, I think you're kind of cute, and the next time, a flutter starts in my stomach. A week later, you're in my thoughts, and then suddenly, all I want is to be in your arms." I relaxed my grip and removed my hand from his mouth and shirt. Would he say he liked me, too? After watching his Adam's apple bob, I pushed out of his arms, rushed up the stairs, and slammed the bedroom door.

At a little before five, I was tired of staring at the ceiling and pretending to sleep. Scrambling out of bed, I grabbed the backpack and tiptoed out of the trailer. I didn't want to hang around and pretend everything was fine. On the driver's seat sat a heart-shaped rock with the word *Believe* etched into the surface. I picked up the stone, and instead of tossing the heart out the window like a child, I stuffed it into my pocket.

Knowing Mom didn't like to get up before nine, I left a message on her phone before driving over. Then, I stood on her front step, pounding for three minutes before she answered.

She opened the door wearing a short, frilly nightshirt. Her now-purple hair stood straight up and smeared mascara made her look like a raccoon.

"What's up?"

"Thought I'd get a jump on the day."

"Fine, but come back in a couple of hours." Mom cocked her head toward the inside of the house. "A friend and I had some brownies last night."

"Never mind. See you next weekend." I watched her shut the door, then quickly placed the stone next to the orange tiger lilies at the front of the house and rushed to the street. Standing beside the car, I turned, retraced my steps, and retrieved the heart.

The winding road did nothing to lighten my mood, but as I rumbled over the cobblestone bricks in Red Hawk's historic downtown district, I felt the heaviness in my chest lighten. This could be the distraction I needed. On previous trips, I had spotted several specialty craft shops, restaurants, and, more importantly, a coffee shop. Today, I was making time to do what I wanted, and the first thing on my list was a latte. Inside, the aroma of fresh-baked pastries surrounded me like a hug. I took my large drink and dark chocolate-filled croissant to a small wooden table beside the plate glass window. I sipped the creamy brew, savoring the warm flakey treat, and watched the sleepy town come awake. Shopkeepers stood outside the vintage downtown buildings from the early nineteen hundreds sweeping sidewalks, setting out chairs, sandwich boards, and water bowls for dogs. I sipped the hot beverage and resisted murmuring, *mmm*, after each bite. When only crumbs remained, I grimaced as a sense of foolishness settled in the pit of my stomach, and I buried my face in my hands. Had I overreacted to Ty's response? The thought of not seeing him clenched my stomach. Why should I miss the beautiful sunsets, campfires, and his company? But if I kept seeing him, when the time came to say goodbye, I'll ugly cry.

The buzzing of my phone drew my attention. I had already declined three of his calls. I answered sternly, without looking at the ID. "Yes."

"Don't use that tone with me." Instead of Ty's voice, Mom's words echoed through the speaker. "Never heard of anyone needing the bakery shop more than you. Not sure what is up, but Ty has been here all morning, ranting about you spiriting him. Knock it off and answer his call."

"The word is ghosting—"

"*Beep-beep-beep.*"

I checked the phone screen. *Disconnected.* Sure enough, Mom hung up on me. *Incoming call.* Flashed on the screen. "Yes."

"Where are you?"

Ty's voice was flat. No anger, annoyance, or concern. Emotionless. "Red Hawk's Coffee on Main. I like their coffee better than yours."

"Don't leave. I'll be there in an hour." He disconnected.

I clenched my teeth to stop from screaming.

The phone buzzed again. Mom.

—You are so good at this distraction. You are totally under Ty's skin. LOL. Be nice.—

After the third time reading the message, I stopped trying to decipher *under Ty's skin*.

Instead of pulling up in his truck, he stopped outside the window on a motorcycle.

Wow! He looked great in a leather jacket and tight jeans. Mustering all my control, I kept my bottom planted on the chair. Did he drive here to tell me no more memorable nights? Or did he talk the lawyer into giving him the bike?

I gazed at the empty cup as the bells above the door jingled.

"What do you recommend? And can I get you a refill?"

I glanced up, and instead of seeing a clenched jaw, I saw a crooked smile creased his face. "A latte with skim milk and any of the bakery items."

He returned with two cups and a breakfast sandwich. "Not much of a sweet guy."

Finding myself tongue-tied, I sipped the latte.

After finishing his food, he bumped into my knee. "So, looks like I'm done working for the day. Let's go shopping. What do you need to start your motorcycle classes?"

How much would a helmet cost, and was there enough in my account?

"Hey." He squeezed my hand. "I took the bike to run the engine."

"It's not that. Payday is Friday, and I'm short on cash."

"Don't worry. I'll subtract the cost from the sale. You agreed on twenty?"

"Twenty-eight thousand!" I could feel the few patrons at the shop staring. I shook my head, only imagining what they thought had me shouting a dollar amount.

"Sal, I was joking. Come on, drink up. Daylight's burning."

The roads along the Mississippi were curvy, full of scenery, and threaded through the quaint towns. The bluffs, river, and scenery attracted lots of motorcycle riders and shops that catered to them. Two blocks from the coffee shop, I followed Ty into a specialty shop. After a lengthy decision about equipment, I walked out with a jacket, gloves, helmet, and a receipt for over five hundred dollars.

"Cheer up. It's only a five-day class, and being safe is important."

"They must sell this stuff by weight. I felt my biceps bulging." I rolled my eyes.

"I can call this all a gift if you do one thing."

"What?" I stopped to catch my breath.

"Go for a ride with me."

I glanced at the cloudless bright-blue sky and knew if the skies were threatening rain, I'd rather spend my day with Ty than at home alone. "Another first. Besides the ride might help me pass the class." I slipped my arms into the black jacket and zipped it.

But before slipping on the helmet, Ty went over the safety rules. "You need to sit close, really close." He winked. "I'll get on first and hold the bike. No sudden shifting, lean with me, and always keep your feet on the pegs. Got it."

Encased by the smell of leather, I exhaled and climbed on behind him. The motorcycle rumbled beneath me. Grinning yet tense, I clung to his waist. As the town disappeared, the bluff came into view, and I released the tension from my shoulders but kept a tight hold on his waist.

He took us through another small town and across the river to Wisconsin. The path went around curvy tree-lined roads, rolling hills, and sweeping curves. Soon, the scenery changed to farmland, rows of corn, soybeans, dotted with red barns, and occasionally cows.

Almost two hours later, he stopped the bike on a hard-packed parking lot with more motorcycles than cars in the middle of nowhere.

Buckle Knuckles. I looked at the name on the sprawling weathered wooden structure.

I climbed off and stretched. So many thoughts tangled my tongue, and I couldn't get the words out. I pulled off the helmet, ran my fingers through my hair, and inhaled. "I'm probably a frightful mess. But wow. The roads, the scenery…"

"Never looked prettier." He leaned over and brushed a light kiss on my cheek.

Why had he kissed me? Did he regret what he said last night? How did I feel? Could I say goodbye in a month? I glanced around but didn't find answers. As we walked past another row of parked motorcycles, I felt a little out of place in my new jacket while admiring those whose sleeves showed crease lines from constant wear and patches of various group names. The people milling about were all ages. Some were clean-shaven, others had long hair and beards, but everyone smiled, waved, or gave a chin nod. Past the parking lot, I spotted an old fire truck surrounded by wooden tables with tractor seats for chairs. Attached to the side of the building were farm tools and metal gas stations and tractor signs.

"What did you think of your first ride?" Ty captured my hand.

"Wow. Love it. Maybe I'll keep the bike."

He scowled. "I shook on the deal."

"Relax. I was only teasing."

"Let's see what they have to eat."

Inside, the theme was similar. Lots of wood, metal signs, memorabilia, and thousands of dollar bills with names and dates scrawled across them tacked on the walls and ceiling. Tabletops constructed from live-edge boards and reclaimed lumber rested on old whiskey barrels. Ty directed me to the only vacant space in the middle of the room beneath a ceiling fan operating on a pulley system. With every turn, I spotted something new. I smiled. Did Bernie want me to have the bike…so I could discover the world is larger than my problems with JR and not everyone judges me? "I like this place."

A woman in her early forties with brown hair tied into a ponytail and a yellow T-shirt with the bar logo walked over. "What can I get you?"

Ty ordered an Arnie Palmer.

I asked her to bring two and wet my lips, anticipating the tea and lemonade drink. As I studied the menu of burgers made from beef, elk, and bison, I saw the scowl on Ty's face.

A moment later, she reappeared with our drinks and took our order.

The lines around Ty's eyes and brows deepened.

"If this is going to be one of those conversations, can you wait until after I eat, and I'm back safe in my car?"

Deep laughter shook his shoulders. He recovered

quickly but continued to grin. "You're so full of surprises. Okay, so how about I talk about your motorcycle classes? Are you ever going to sign up?"

"Again, waiting for payday. What your dad neglected to tell you was besides getting the life sucked out of me, JR drained my bank account." I shook my head. "Don't say it. I was a fool, but I wasn't the only one. He fooled government officials into giving him highway contracts, forged bonds, brought in new investors, and—"

Ty cast his gaze to the left. "Looks like she's bringing our burgers."

I quieted my racing heart as she approached with an elk and bison burger, cheese curds, and sweet potato fries.

Receiving a decline on refills, she left us with the food and a promise to check back.

"He sounds like a jerk, and I'll happily pay for the class. After all, it's for my benefit."

"Thanks, and just because I am feeling really kindhearted, I'll let you pick up the tab for lunch."

"Gladly. So, what do you say to sharing?" He positioned the knife above his burger.

As a response, I chopped my elk burger in half. Halfway through lunch, I still couldn't decide if I liked one sandwich more than the other, but I liked the fresh curds Barb had better than the deep-fried presented with lunch. After the meal, I walked through the attached gift shop, admiring the biker apparel and accessories, before heading to the parking lot.

Ty climbed on the bike. "Ready?"

"Do you think you could take the long way back?" I smiled. "Only because the bike needs to be driven.

The motor needs to be run."

"Sure thing."

After the bike stopped in Red Hawk, I climbed off the back, and all the anger and humiliation I had been dragging around for the past few years was missing. I took an easy breath, expanding my lungs.

Ty stepped from the bike. "Looks like the ride was good for you. There is something freeing about being on a bike. Dad always said a therapist was expensive, but wind therapy was free."

"He was a smart man." I tugged the zipper on my jacket. "Thank you—"

"I needed this time with you on the bike." He pulled me in for a hug.

Even though things remained unsaid, and I didn't receive a kiss goodbye, I felt hopeful. Did Ty have a different love language?

Chapter Nine

On Monday morning, when I checked my phone, I spotted a text from Mom. I rolled my eyes. Had she been eating bakery treats?

—*If you're not the reason, Ty was grinning and singing when he put the bike in the garage last night. Let me know. I'll kick his pretty little behind.*—

I sent a screenshot of the message to Ty, along with the cost of the class.

He immediately paid through a cash app, sending a receipt, a slew of emojis with praying hands, and a request.

—*Please let your mom know you're the reason for me being happy. She packs a punch.*—

After a thumbs-up response, I went to the kitchen, opened the refrigerator, and pondered my options for lunch. A carton of skim milk, catsup, mustard, mayo, and three varieties of hot sauce. Somehow, grocery shopping had slipped my mind. Luckily, I had a loaf of bread stashed in the freezer. After chipping off a couple of slices, I moved to the bedroom. Looking through my closet, I realized I needed to wash clothes. After deciding not to pick the cleanest shirt from the hamper, I chose from the assortment of slacks, blouses, and dresses that had hung in the craft room closet untouched for over two years.

Standing tall, I rifled through the hangers. I found

my favorite business casual attire and slipped on light gray linen pants and a white, stretch cotton, fitted shirt. Before returning to the kitchen, I grabbed a pair of black leather slides. I laughed at being overdressed while plastering crunchy peanut butter across the slightly thawed multigrain bread. Putting the sandwich into my purse, I found the heart-shaped stone imprinted with *Believe.* I placed the rock in the center of the table, changed my mind, and slipped it back. Out of all the rocks I found, this one brought me the most comfort, and I wanted to keep it near, almost like a lucky charm.

Joe and Lisa would immediately notice my attire, but the other phone reps wouldn't give me a second glance until a call went unanswered.

Then, the associates would turn and glare until I picked up the phone.

I didn't think any of them knew my name. To them, I was a cranky middle-aged woman answering phones. They'd had no idea once I had been the administrative assistant to the owner of multi-million-dollar firms that oversaw the completion of numerous roadway construction projects. If Old Man Sumpter wouldn't have welcomed back his wayward son...damn JR.

In the small lunchroom at work, I poured black coffee into my ceramic cup and inhaled the strong, bitter brew. The half-empty glass pot sputtered and crackled when I sat it back on the burner plate.

Joe yanked the refrigerator door open. "Do you have a job interview? Or are you meeting someone?"

Shaking my head, I retrieved the sandwich and an outdated pudding cup.

He placed the food on the third shelf and shut the

door. "You're taking the news better than I thought."

"Joe, you're rambling." I stepped closer, articulating my words. "Are you having a stroke? Smile so I can see if your face is lopsided."

As he drew his eyebrows together, he made eye contact but didn't smile.

I tightened my stomach and waited for a gut punch. "What happened?"

"They released JR from prison on Friday."

"What!" Thoughts collided like cars on black ice in the dead of winter. I could barely stammer my next question. "No. He has a three-year—"

"In Minnesota, you only need to serve two-thirds of the sentence before gaining supervised release." I dug my fingers into his arm. "He can't be out. Wouldn't someone have to tell me?"

Joe pried my hand loose. "It was fraud, forgery, and money laundering, not violent crimes. Besides, the money wasn't yours."

"How can you say that? I was vested in the construction firm and worked for them for over twenty years. Besides my pension, I lost my car, engagement ring, bank account, and good name." With trembling limbs, I reached for the chair and sat. The sensation of falling was what I imagined people felt when their plane dropped from the sky, except I didn't crash. I fell endlessly.

"Sorry. I'm stupid." He hung his head and peered up at me.

"How could you not tell me? I thought the two of us were friends."

"You had the day off, and I didn't want to spoil your fun. So, I figured I'd wait until Monday." He rested a hand on my shoulder.

I brushed him away and picked up my cup of coffee. So many thoughts. Was I mad at Joe or the government for releasing JR? I moved behind the desk and noticed Joe had followed. I pointed to my blinking message light. "First temps above eighties, the phones are already ringing."

"They say it's not good to bottle things up."

Scowling with my eyebrows drawn low and the right side of my mouth quivering, I watched him scurry away. After listening to the first message in the queue, I rolled my eyes. The call center would be short-staffed by two representatives today. Most of the time, I didn't mind the extra work and appreciated being busy, but the news of JR's release scattered my thoughts and sapped my energy. The morning flew by, and the rumbling in my stomach grew louder, leaving me no choice but to eat lunch. I stepped into the lunchroom and spotted Joe and Lisa already sitting at a table.

Joe pointed. "You can see why I was confused. She looks like a fashionista."

With clenched teeth, I grabbed my sandwich from the refrigerator and sat next to Lisa.

A blonde woman in her early forties bustled through the entrance, wearing a fitted pale-green linen dress with stylish white work pumps. "Allow me to introduce myself, Karen Miller, Human Resource Director."

"Sally, phone rep." After taking a bite of my mangled peanut butter sandwich, I realized I should have stood and shook her hand. Too late now. I took another bite while the others introduced themselves.

Karen sat in the remaining chair. "Sally, I have

been going through employee files. Is that a Saint Lourey shirt?"

Something about the tone in her voice and the way her gaze continued to go over my attire set me on edge. Not bothering to finish lunch, I quickly nodded, stood, and refilled my coffee cup. "Got to get back. The call center is short-staffed, again."

Before I could walk away, I caught Lisa giving me a death stare. I shrugged and hustled back. As soon as I sat, I watched the woman to my right sign off the phones and mouthed *bye*. Thirty minutes later, callers had backed up in the queue.

Mr. Smith, the company president, walked past with Karen.

She nodded.

With headphones, all I could do was watch their mouths moving. The twisting of my stomach caused me to wince. Would Karen investigate me? Did she already know I not only managed the office for the company that made headlines two years ago, but I also was engaged to the man who toppled his daddy's empire?

The caller huffed through the phone and mumbled, "Can't hire good help."

"Yes, I am still here, and again I apologize. The scheduling page still hasn't loaded. I should write a book with conversational tidbits to fill the void while waiting for computers to load."

The customer chuckled. "Just don't mention the weather. It's all Minnesotans talk about."

Somehow, five o'clock came, and I eagerly switched the phones to voice mail with the prerecorded message on who to call in an emergency.

Out in the parking lot, Joe and Lisa paced around

my vehicle.

"What are you guys up to now?"

Joe smiled. "The two of us decided you need company tonight."

"I don't feel like going out, but if you want to come over."

"Perfect, I'll swing by the Chinese King." Lisa nodded.

"I'll get wine." Joe grinned with a gleam in his eyes.

At least, I'd have a few minutes to straighten my bedroom and kitchen before they arrived. As I walked through the door, I heard my phone buzz. I didn't recognize the caller ID and declined the call. A moment later, I received a text from Ty.

—*When do your classes start? Is it safe for me to head over to your mom's house?*—

A text came from the number I declined.

—*Sally, call me back, now! Please!*—

With trembling fingers, I took a screenshot of the message before deleting the text. Was the message random spam or JR? Before I could respond to Ty, I heard knocking on my door and rushed to let them inside. "Welcome." I pointed. "This way to the kitchen."

The small area had enough room for a wooden table pushed against the white wall and three chairs with matching red cushions I had sewn. "I think JR tried to contact me?" I sat.

"Just relax, I've got this." Joe searched through the cupboards for the wine glasses.

Lisa grabbed the yellow sunflower plates and utensils and pulled the food from the large paper bag.

"Thanks, my hands are shaking." I held them up. "Why would he want to talk after all this time?"

"Are you sure?" Joe screwed the top off a bottle of sparkling chardonnay and filled our glasses.

I showed him the screenshot of the text. "The call I assumed was spam, but after declining, I got the text, and I have a gut feeling it's JR."

Lisa opened the top of the white boxes, and scented steam filled the air. "Can you go to the police and ask them to issue a restraining order?"

"Just block JR's number." Joe *tsked* and rolled his eyes.

I nodded. "Yeah, I know it's not a crime to call someone. But I keep thinking why and did he call anyone else?" I dropped a scoop of sticky rice onto my plate, along with a heaping spoonful from each of the remaining boxes. Beef and broccoli with oyster sauce, Kung Pao, and orange chicken crowded my plate. I speared a pea pod and red pepper with my fork. The first bite was crunchy, salty, and tangy. "Thanks, I can't believe I can eat."

Halfway through the meal, Joe raised his glass. "To friends, lousy exes, and our new HR director."

Lisa stopped before she could clink glasses. "I will not toast to Karen. She told me older employees are raising the rates of health insurance."

"What is wrong with her?" I retracted my arm as my phone buzzed. I reached over and turned on the speaker. "Hi, Mom. What's up?"

"Ty didn't show up today. Does he know I'm going to whoop—"

"I think he's helping Travis with rocks. You're on speaker, and I'm eating with a couple of co-workers."

"Okay, but before I go, tell me."

"Yes, I put a smile on his face. Also, they released JR from prison, so don't answer any calls from unknown numbers. I'll talk to you later." I disconnected and emptied half the wine from my glass as heat singed my cheeks. "So, do you want the long or short story?"

Joe refilled the glasses.

Lisa shook her head. "Did you tell him you loved him?"

"The only thing I said was, *if this isn't love,* and he cut me off with the old tired line, *it's not you, it's me.* Can you believe it?"

Joe cocked his head. "So, after that, you put a smile on his—"

"No, I went to bed alone and snuck out of the camper before he awoke."

Joe leaned forward. "Your reaction was a little over the top. But I'm smart enough not to ask if this response was hormonal."

"Why is Ty happy?" Lisa socked him in the arm.

I got to the point, explained about the motorcycle ride, and how we left things unsaid.

Lisa and I stared at nothing.

Joe jumped into action. He put away leftovers and placed dishes in the dishwasher. Fifteen minutes later, he sat. "You knew this would not end well. He was always going to leave. You have two options. Enjoy what's left of the summer with Ty, or have fun without him. But don't think if you love him, you can change him."

"There is a third possibility. Ask him if he wants company on his travels." Lisa tapped her right index finger against the empty glass.

"Are you drunk?" I glared. "There is no way I could afford to take a year off work."

Lisa laughed and pointed at the bottle. "It's a non-alcoholic. Joe has embraced the sober-ish trend. Only two drinks per week, and apparently, he didn't want to waste his real drinks with us. Next time, I'm not sending Joe for the booze."

"What is this?" Joe grabbed a stone off the table, flipping the rock over. He held the heart up to the light.

"Ever since Wendy died, I have been finding heart-shaped objects."

Lisa exchanged glances with Joe.

"Do not fill my workstation with hearts."

Joe stood and retrieved my crystal flutes, dessert plates, fortune cookies, and a bottle of champagne. He filled the glasses. "A toast with the real stuff. To friends, adventure, love, and Wendy."

After three clinks, Lisa tapped the edge of the fluted glassware against the rock. "Wendy, I want the heart you send me to be in the chest of a willing man." She opened her cookie. "The love of your life will appear unexpectedly."

"Your smile brings happiness to everyone you meet." He tilted his head like a dog, looking to be rewarded.

I crossed the fingers in my left hand, hoping I wouldn't read anything about unexpected visitors. "Life awaits. That's stupid, but at least the fortune didn't say death was at my doorstep."

Alone, I sprawled out on the bed, completed the class registration, and texted Ty.

—I start on Wednesday night, and if I pass the permit test, motorcycle training is on Saturday. I won't

be able to come this weekend.—

He responded almost at once.

—Great news. I shoveled rocks for Travis all day. Of course, he scheduled the delivery for when he was at work. I think having Amber as the agent would have been a better choice—

—I think I missed something. Now, you want Amber to sell the house?—

He sent back a *LOL* and then called to let me know Travis had agreed not to list the house with Amber. Mom could stay until she found an apartment. Then his voice rose an octave as he explained he could leave as soon as he had the bike title.

With a dozen conflicting thoughts, the words muffled. Was he in that big of a hurry to get away from me?

He kept going on and on about how everything worked out. He no longer had to deal with Amber. Even though he had no desire to resume things, he disliked being around her and remembering himself as his worst version.

I swallowed down the bitterness and hoped I would sound cheery and supportive. I told him about JR's release and the strange text message.

"Is the man dangerous? Are your doors locked?"

Through the airwaves, I heard concern in his voice as he continued to fire questions, not pausing long enough for me to answer. I interrupted. "JR is only interested in money, and I have none. But his dad still does. They cleared Old Man Sumpter of all charges."

"Sally! He wants you to call. Why? You ruled out finances. What else?"

Pacing as the silence hung between us, I couldn't

think of a reason. Picking the heart from the table, I fingered the soft material. "It doesn't matter. I blocked his number."

After saying goodbye, uneasiness settled over me. I called Mom and told her about the motorcycle ride, classes, and the odd message. "If JR steps a foot on my property, I'll run a broomstick up his rear end and make him sweep the sidewalk."

I disconnected and wondered why I even bothered worrying about the tough old bird.

****

Wednesday night before leaving for class, I slipped the stone from my purse and ran an index finger across the word *believe*. The classroom contained a handful of teenage boys, an instructor in his fifties, and me. He used slides, videos, and the whiteboard to go over all the terms and questions on the test.

After two hours, I took an online permit test. The digital clock on the screen counted down the questions remaining as I clicked on the answers, my confidence growing with each scenario presented. When I hit the submit button, I leaned back, feeling a wave of relief and satisfaction. But then I glanced around and noticed I was the only one done. *Did I rush things?*

The instructor motioned for me to approach his desk.

I stood and trudged to the front of the room, hoping I wouldn't have to repeat the class.

He smiled and gave a head nod. "The DMV will email the official results. Bring a printed copy of the permit to class on Saturday."

After smiling and thanking him, I raced to my car. and texted Ty.

—I have a motorcycle permit.—

On Saturday, I had sweaty palms and shaky knees. I drove into the designated area and parked by the other vehicles. Walking toward a group of adults, I noticed a section of the lot with orange cones and twelve identical motorcycles. I exhaled. The bikes were a lot smaller than Bernie's. Nothing flashy, very basic. A white painted course with circles, figure-eights, a traffic lane with an intersection, and a stop sign. As I waited for the class to begin, I discovered four of the twelve students were women who had previously obtained permits and skipped the classroom portion.

The instructors introduced themselves. Bob and Teddy had been riding bikes for over forty years.

Teddy had silver hair and a bushy beard.

Bob was clean-shaven with a salt-and-pepper braid hanging to his waist.

The instructors spent the first hour going over the parts of the motorcycle.

The last hour, I spent riding. Struggling with shifting I continually killed the motorcycle engine. Then I put the bike in the wrong gear, and when I kick-started the bike, the motor revved, and I almost lost my balance.

Bob and Teddy took turns being encouraging. At the end of the session, Bob walked over. "Don't worry, you're not the worst student. Once, I had a student drive their bike into the trailer, and another time the kid ran over my foot. You'll get the hang of shifting, I promise."

After class, the first person I called was Ty. "I drove a 250cc black motorcycle and didn't crash."

"Yeah, yeah. That's nice."

Musical laughter and the buzz of conversation echoed through the phone speaker.

I tensed. Was that a woman's voice? Where was he? "If you're busy, then I can let you go."

"No, I've got time. Let me step outside. Wish I was there with you." He sighed.

The strain in his voice made me want to reach through the phone and wrap my arms around him. "I wish you were here, too. Sounds like you're not having any fun."

"Two weeks wasted helping with the damn fence."

I heard the top of a soda or beer can open and a few more sighs. Waiting for him to continue, I sorted laundry. Long pauses in the conversation were not unusual for Ty.

He swallowed.

I shut the lid on my stackable washer in the hall closet next to the kitchen.

"They broke up. Travis wanted to move into the trailer with me. I said *no*. So, he's moving in with your mom."

I wasn't sure how to respond, but I was happy I wouldn't be sharing the camper with Travis. However, I was worried about the outcome. What if the two couldn't get along and Mom wanted to move in with me? I'd no longer have a reason to drive and see Ty each weekend, and he'd be under no obligation to stay. After hearing several heavy sighs and a vehicle door slamming. I thought I heard a woman laughing. "Does Travis have a new girlfriend?"

"No, that was Amber. She's like a shadow. I can't turn around without bumping into her. All she wants is to reminisce about the good old days, and she remembers them more fondly than I ever did."

He's honest and not hiding anything, so that's a good sign. A long slow breath whistled between my teeth as I slumped onto the floor. "Guess the two of us have had better weeks. But on the bright side, I haven't had to block any more numbers, and I'm still employed. Karen, the new director of HR, doesn't like me. She told me I was over-dressed and underperforming. So, now my only references would come from an ex-con and her."

Ten minutes later, I said goodbye and tried to shake the jealousy that took hold of the mental images of Amber and Ty. She probably wouldn't care if he was leaving at the end of the summer. Besides, she occupied a part of his youth. Was she his first? Should I drive to Wisconsin? I struggled from the floor and started the washer. I knew how things would end. Tightness closed my throat, and I brushed back a tear. Ty would leave, and I'd be stuck working at a go-nowhere job. He and I wanted different things. Maybe next weekend, I'd look for a dog.

On Sunday, after brewing coffee, I headed to the craft room to work on the quilt I was donating to the animal shelter for their silent auction. I searched through boxes for my rotary cutter and mat. By the time the sun set, blue, green, and yellow triangles littered the floor. I stood, stretched, and tried to ease the cramps in my neck. I rearranged the squares, and a vague emptiness zapped my energy. The hum of the needle racing across the fabric no longer made me smile. The tip of my index finger found a straight pin. Wincing, I yanked back my finger before a drop of blood stained the fabric, my previous melancholy was replaced by a quick surge of adrenaline. I searched for a bandage, wondering why I had thought quilting was fun.

With the sunlight fading to dark, I got undressed, wondering how Ty's day had gone. Was Amber still helping? Had Travis moved in, or had he reconciled with his girlfriend? I tugged on a nightshirt as my phone vibrated across the bed. "Hello."

"Nice to hear your voice again. I'm a little disappointed you didn't visit me in jail."

The pounding in my eardrums drowned out JR's voice.

Chapter Ten

On Monday morning, after very little sleep, I zombie-walked into Smith and Son's Heating and Air Conditioning. Before receiving JR's call Sunday night, I had thought the apartment building was quiet. Yet last night, I heard footsteps echoing down the halls, and the people above me sounded like they were clogging. I bumped into Joe in the lunchroom. "Hey."

"You look spent. Rough night?"

"JR called me last night. What if he shows up at work? The last thing I need is for Karen to ask questions." I sighed. "Last night, I started thinking about why JR would want to talk. At the trial, he claimed a third party improperly accessed the million dollars transferred to creditors. The prosecuting attorneys investigated and found no evidence of unauthorized access or hacking. They maintained that the misdirection of funds was an insider job, and JR had accessed the email accounts. Do you think he hid something in my possessions?"

"Doubtful. Forensic accountants could find the money, or at least the cash."

Karen walked into the lunchroom wearing a black blazer, skirt, and blouse. "Morning. Aren't you a cheery group?" She glanced at my attire of leggings, T-shirt, and flip-flops. "Should be another busy day. Mr. Smith and I agreed to introduce productivity standards for the call center. Evidence…"

I cringed. Did Karen toss out *evidence* because she knows about my past with JR? I smiled and picked up the cup of coffee. "Looking forward to seeing the new job description with the standards listed. Will the salary be based on comparable worth? Tech support positions would be the equivalent to a call center support staff." I exited, huffing like an out-of-shape runner going uphill. I should have kept my mouth shut, but after hearing JR's voice last night, I was on edge and not thinking clearly. To keep this job, I needed to be nice to Karen, not alienate her.

Of course, as luck would have it, Karen ate lunch with us.

She said something about wanting us to feel like a team.

For thirty minutes, the four of us talked about the weather, TV shows, and movies.

And no matter the subject, Karen sprinkled, *we are one company into the conversation.*

Walking back to my desk, I heard a Johnny Paycheck song, and the lyrics "Take this Job and Shove It" became an earworm for the rest of the day. After work, I headed to class for my second night of instruction. I did better at shifting, and instead of being a nervous wreck, I enjoyed my time riding. When I got home, the sun had set, and I was starving. I raced up the stairs to my apartment and devoured an oversized bowl of my childhood favorite cereal, chocolate balls, without milk. The crunching eased frustration over Ty not calling, JR's intrusion, and Karen's insensitive comments. Whoever said you couldn't eat your feelings had never experienced the therapeutic power of crunching.

I changed into my nightshirt and sent a generic message to Ty. I didn't want him to think I was checking up on him, even though I was.

—Nightly update: practice went better tonight than work. How was your day?—

If he didn't respond, the next person I'd call was Mom to see if she'd seen him with Amber.

The phone buzzed.

I double-checked the ID. "Hey."

"Hope you don't mind talking. I set my readers down. I think they're at your mom's."

"You have cheaters?" Why didn't he know where they were? Had he been visiting Travis or Amber?

His laughter rumbled. "I usually wear contacts."

"Did you work at the house?"

"It took us all until midnight on Sunday to get the bedroom prepared for Travis. I patched the holes, removed the carpet, and installed a closet organizer. What a difference. The bedroom looks larger, and the closet is functional. If the rest of the house comes together like this…getting top dollar shouldn't be a problem. Without Amber helping at the house—"

"Oh. What happened to Amber being annoying, a constant shadow, and someone who only wanted to talk about the past?" Had his feelings changed? I clenched my jaw to stop myself from saying anymore.

"She's still bothersome, but she also has an eye for style, design, and color. I couldn't have gotten the room done without her. Next weekend, when Travis isn't sleeping with us in the trailer, you'll thank her, too."

I'd rather thank her for staying away from Ty. "I got a call from JR."

"What did he want?" His voice was louder and slightly higher.

Did I make a mistake telling him? "Something stupid. Surprised I didn't visit him in jail."

"People change."

Clenching the phone tighter, I watched my knuckles turn white. Was he referring to Amber, JR, or himself? I faked a yawn. "Just wanted to say hi. I'm really tired and have to get up early. Bye."

"Yeah. Goodnight."

"Night." I disconnected. As soon as the glow from the phone faded, I tried to mute my racing thoughts. I looked through the list of calls received and hit redial. After the fifth ring, JR's voice vibrated through the speaker.

"Good to see some things don't change. After blocking me, you call. You are the most confusing woman—"

"Why did you call?" I tried to keep my voice flat and emotionless.

"Did you think about me while I was gone? Miss me?"

I exhaled. "You have ten seconds to answer. Ten, nine—"

"To make amends. I love you, Sally."

Clenching the phone harder, I gritted my teeth. How dare he say he loved me? I took a deep breath. "Anything else?"

"Sal, don't be like this. I made some mistakes. I love—"

Not wanting to hear anymore, I disconnected and blocked his number. How had I ever imagined myself in love with him? Had I been so desperate for attention or blinded by his words? Again, I shifted through the events in the past, trying to see where I went wrong.

The next few days, the weather mimicked my mood—overcast skies with rainy evenings. The instructors rescheduled for Saturday. Ty and I had exchanged a few texts during the week, mostly greetings. By Thursday, I was restless and called Mom, but she didn't answer. A little concerned I hadn't heard from her all week, I called Ty.

"What's up?"

Not expecting to hear those words, I tensed. Was I intruding? Did he think I was checking up on him? "Mom hasn't answered my calls. They emailed the new schedule for classes and the test. I won't be able to come for three weeks. I could reschedule for this fall."

"No, don't quit. You could still get a motorcycle endorsement by the end of July. I can manage the remodeling without your help."

I grounded my molars, forcing my words between clenched teeth. Not one word about missing me or being disappointed in not going for a motorcycle ride together. Was Amber taking my place on the back of the bike? "Have you seen my mom recently? She's not returning my calls."

His laughter rumbled. "Mabel, it's your daughter, and she's worried about you."

After a bit of rustling of the phone, her voice cracked. "Sal, I'm fine. I forgot my phone at home and spent the last couple of days at the camper while the floor in my bedroom dries. Have you seen the sunset over the river? Just a second. What's that, Amber? Yeah, yeah. Got to go." She disconnected.

Clenching the phone tighter, I waited for Ty to

return the call. Instead of feeling relief that Mom was safe, I fumed.

I arrived early at work on Friday, hoping to talk Joe and Lisa into coming over. Of course, they both had plans. Everyone had a social life but me. The thought of driving to Wisconsin on Sunday twisted my gut. Would I be an unwanted guest at Ty's trailer and Mom's house? I should have asked if Trevor was still living with her.

On Sunday, I sewed blue binding on the quilt for the No-Kill Animal Shelter annual auction. The only thing I had left to do was press it.

Searching through my storage buckets for some white tissue paper to place between the folds, I found a stash of material—lots of warm autumn colors. I began cutting out the squares, imagining Ty crawling under the cover. He might not be staying, but when he leaves, he'll take a part of me. The thought oddly comforted me. I wished Ty wanted the same things I did...a home, a dog, sharing dinner, and weekend getaways.

As I arranged the squares, I thought about JR. He had been such a supporter of animal shelters. Every year, he donated expensive gifts for the auction. I had talked about getting a puppy, but JR insisted I wait until he had a fence installed around the yard. Why did he have to be a life wrecker? He seemed to care, but were all the words and gestures an act? I rubbed my chest and remembered all the sorrow and pain reflected in the receptionist's eyes. She had just bought a house and was expecting a baby. Then the hopelessness displayed in the diesel mechanics and heavy equipment operators as JR's father announced, with tears, the start of a federal inquiry. Sumpter Construction would close its doors and file for bankruptcy. Shivers raced up my spine, as I remembered the crushing feeling of knowing the employees would still have jobs if I hadn't instigated the investigation.

I cringed as my thoughts continued down the rutted roads. Would Karen fire me for not meeting call center standards? I knew the younger women were more efficient at answering calls. They never made idle chatter. But Wendy liked how I never rushed a caller. She thought making our customers feel like friends and family was more important than the quantity of calls.

After cutting, pinning, and stitching my fears and worries away for hours, I stood and stretched. Between sewing and riding, everything ached. I checked the time as being a little after three, too early to get ready for bed. I stuffed my wallet into my weekend backpack and headed to the store. The way things were going, I needed something to grind between my teeth besides sugary cereals.

The market was less than a mile away and only two city blocks from the public walking path. I stepped outside and filled my lungs. Another thunderstorm would roll in that evening, but for now, I'd be okay. The fresh air was nice after being cooped up indoors.

Following the sidewalk, I noticed an array of utility markings of blue, yellow, and orange spray paint. In the summer, construction crews were constantly digging something up. I passed the parking lot and stepped onto the shaded trail. Oak, ash, maple, and elm trees lined the path. The overhead branches created a canopy of green to walk under. In the fall, orange, yellow, and red leaves would carpet the blacktop trial.

I slowed my steps. Would Ty leave as soon as he

had the bike, or would he wait until the first snow? I shook my head. First, I had to pass the driving test. I slipped the phone from my back pocket and texted Ty.

—*The instructors are trying to arrange things so I can take the motorcycle test next Saturday.*—

Before hitting Send, I searched my emojis and chose one with fingers crossed.

"Hey." A voice rumbled behind me.

I veered to the right, thinking a jogger wanted to pass. Suddenly, a sweaty hand grasped my arm, and a jolt of terror raced through me. The pounding of my heart fed my fear. Too frightened to run, I stood with the fine hair on my forearm vibrating. *JR?* I drew in a shaky breath and turned to confront my stalker. Deep creases etched my forehead as I pulled my eyebrows together. Snorting, I brushed aside the woman's hand. She was thirty years older, two inches shorter, fifty pounds heavier, and I had no idea why she grabbed me.

With scuff marks marring her white orthopedic tennis shoes and sweat staining the armpits on her multi-colored flowered T-shirt, she tipped from the waist, panting like an overworked dog.

Slipping an arm around her sweaty shirt, I propelled her to a park bench. "Sit." After watching her comply, I, too, plopped on the worn wooden bench.

The color in her cheeks changed from an over-ripened tomato to a pasty white. She loosened her hold on my arm.

"Are you going to be okay? Do you need me to call someone?"

With a crooked finger, she motioned to come closer. "Are you Sal?" She nodded.

I peered through her finger-smudged eyeglasses

into tired eyes. "Why?"

"He said you were and gave me two hundred dollars to give this to you." She pulled a white letter-sized envelope from an unseen pocket on her shirt. Crumpled, yet sealed.

I recognized the logo from Sumpter Construction.

"Please." She waved the crumpled packet. "If you don't take it, then I'll need to return the money. I wanted to surprise Muffy with a new bed and some tasty treats."

"Muffy?" I could feel my resolve melt at the thought of some poor critter.

"My fluffy, little muffin rescue." Her gaze widened. "Don't tell management. I got a kitten. They'll want a pet deposit and fifty dollars more a month."

"You live in my complex?"

"Yeah, first floor by the entrance. I see everyone. That's why the man showed me your picture and asked about you."

If I didn't know how persuasive and charming JR could be, I would have yelled at this woman for putting her health at risk. I hadn't even been walking that fast or that far. She clearly needed more exercise than monitoring the residents.

She pushed the envelope in front of me. "I don't care what you do with the mail, but you need to take the letter."

"Fine." I stuffed it into the side pocket of my backpack. "I was walking to the store, but I'll take you home."

"I'm fine, but could you pick up a few things for me, too? I can pay." She reached down the front of her shirt and pulled a roll of twenty-dollar bills from what I assumed was her bra.

I accepted the money and made a mental note to wash my hands. With the added responsibility of kitty treats, bread, and potato chips with ridges, I started walking and felt the buzz from my phone. Instead of being eager to chat with Ty, shivers shook my spine. Hesitantly, I removed the phone and checked the message.

—*We will have to celebrate. Can you take a day off? I could make an appointment with the attorney and get the title transferred. Miss you.*—

Would Ty still be interested after I gave him the bike? How would he respond if I told him I might want to keep the bike for a year? I replied with a happy face emoji before entering the grocery store and staring vacantly at the advertised specials. *Why did I come?* I walked down the aisles, and when I saw a cat food display, everything came rushing back...JR, cat lady, and my frustration. After grabbing a loaf of bread, I proceeded to a display of pre-cut vegetables and tossed a few bags into my cart, along with a container of hummus.

I left the store weighed down by my backpack and clutching the handles of two plastic bags. When I reached the apartment, I had a sweaty shirt and arms that felt like soggy noodles. Struggling, I lifted my arm high enough to knock on the door.

The door eased open. Cat Lady poked her head out with a phone pressed against her ear.

I set the bag down and headed upstairs to my apartment. *Was she talking to JR?* I inserted the key into my door and hesitated. She'll need to know about his criminal record...the loser, preying on sweet, unsuspecting Cat Lady. After tossing a few things into the refrigerator, I raced back downstairs.

She invited me inside to see the cat, who refused to come from under her bed.

I told her about the No-Kill Shelter and the upcoming auction. I declined a coffee and cautioned her about taking money from strangers, especially a just-released felon.

"He was so kind and nice." She furrowed her brow. "Are you sure?"

For thirty minutes, I explained how I worked for the company JR's father owned, and I had to go to court and testify against JR regarding his criminal activity. I watched her nod as she wrinkled her brow. I stood because I couldn't think of anything else to say to convince her. "Take my phone number. If he contacts you, call me." *What is JR up to?* I paced. *Will he contact my mom next? Show up at work? Should I be working on getting a gun permit instead of a motorcycle license?*

****

On Monday, I pushed aside the dread of knowing I'd spend the day counting down the hours until I could switch off the phones. Things were better with Wendy. She always had special projects and valued my opinions. But Karen's only focus was productivity. Scowling, I pushed through the doors into the office.

But today, Joe didn't greet me. In the lunchroom, I found a note taped to the coffee machine. *Management will no longer supply coffee.*

I slumped back to my desk with water splashing in my cup. Monday just got worse. I texted Joe.

—What's up?—

—Read the company email.—

Leaning back in my chair, I scanned the correspondence. *A feasibility company was conducting a study, and everyone should cooperate with any request for information.*

Did Karen convince the owners she could save them money by outsourcing? The thought of looking for a job twisted my stomach. At lunch, I stepped into the vacant lunchroom. From now on, no one would want to take the time away from their desk for fear and risk of being labeled unnecessary. After grabbing my sandwich, I rushed to my car and slipped behind the wheel. Did the curtains in Karen's office move? I drove to the nearest gas station, where I bought a large iced coffee from their food and snack station and texted Ty.

—I miss you.—

—Miss you more. Want to get dinner in Lake View City on Tuesday? It's only a forty-five-minute drive for you. I could get a room at the historic hotel with a river view.—

I included a dozen happy face emojis with *yes* in caps. When I returned from lunch, I brought two additional iced coffees and placed them on Joe's and Lisa's desk before clocking back into the phone system. The tension in the office was palpable. A rash of installers called in sick, and to accommodate the angry customers without air conditioning, I readjusted schedules. Of course, my numbers would be horrific with the hold times increasing for customers. The churning in my stomach intensified by the minute, and I, too, thought about calling in sick. All I needed was to get through Tuesday, and I'd be wrapping my arms around Ty.

Before heading to work, I packed some essentials. The last thing I needed was to show up on Wednesday wearing the same clothes as Tuesday. I grinned. However, that might get Joe to leave his office. I felt like a kid on Halloween, knowing I'd be satisfied by the time the sun set—but with kisses and tender caresses instead of candy.

At work, I stepped into the lunchroom, tossed my sandwich into the refrigerator, and caught the scent of freshly brewed coffee. I turned and sighed.

"Sal, I'm glad I caught you." Karen held an extra-large cup of coffee. "I wanted you to know the company has adopted the standard of eighty-twenty."

I shrugged and shifted my gaze between the sink and her steamy cup.

"You probably weren't aware since you have no prior call center experience. I read through your file and application. Let me explain." Her white teeth flashed. "I expect you to answer eighty percent of all calls within twenty seconds."

"Thanks for the information." I pushed past her, even with lips pressed firmly together, "We're all one team" slipped out of my mouth. Thirty feet from my desk, I inhaled. Java. I rushed to the workstation and grinned like a proud mother at the large paper cup with chocolate-covered-espresso-bean on the plastic cover and a note card—*Compliments of Joe.*

At five, I signed off the phone and quickly calculated my service level. I groaned. I had only answered sixty-five percent of the incoming calls within thirty seconds. At least, I hadn't had another Karen sighting and was still employed.

Chapter Eleven

On Tuesday, as soon as I stepped into the lobby of the historic hotel in Lake View City, the tension in my shoulders eased. The polished wooden floor, tapestry rugs, fireplace, and faint coffee scent added a touch of warmth. The dark paneling, the stained-glass lighting, the leather wing chairs, and the end tables with their soft, glowing lamps all beckoned me to sit and relax, creating a welcoming atmosphere. I couldn't help but smile at the gentleman in his dark suit, standing before the small wooden cubbies with room numbers and keys.

"Sal?" Ty's deep voice rumbled.

Before turning to greet him, I caught my reflection in the window, white shorts, a blue T-shirt, and sandals. Why didn't I choose a dress? Feeling frumpy and embarrassed, I turned.

He met my gaze with a slow smile and took measured steps.

The softness around his eyes and the warmth of his smile had me feeling like a princess in a childhood tale. I had never felt more beautiful. How much time had passed since his lips captured mine?

Ty stopped just before reaching me. "Sal, you look beautiful. Stunning. I could stand here all day."

Instead of rushing into his arms, I stood, taking in the sight of him, as the subtle scent of his cologne teased my senses. The curve of his lips had me aching for a kiss.

He rushed forward and drew me closer.

I tangled my fingers in the short curls at the nape of his neck and clutched his shirt. After sharing a passionate kiss, I no longer wondered if Ty had missed me.

"Come on." His voice was husky as he slung my backpack onto his shoulder in one fluid movement.

The room was quaint, with a patchwork flowered quilt, an oak four-poster bed, and windows overlooking the river's swell, but I wasn't interested in the view.

Ty trailed kisses down my neck, murmuring, "I missed you."

I unfastened two buttons before tracing the tan line on his chest. "You must have been wearing only T-shirts the last couple of weeks."

"Maybe I'll spend the winter at a nude beach and get rid of my tan lines."

Wind rattled the windowpanes, mimicking the fear twitching in my gut at the thought of him leaving. "The weather channel has been predicting storms all day. I guess it's blowing in now. Looks like I'll be stuck indoors. Any ideas on what I can do?"

"Hmmm." His hands fluttered over my back. "I have been working hard. A back rub might be nice."

I finished unbuttoning his shirt. The room grew dark, and rain pelted the windows. A second later, the first flash lit up the room, casting shadows on the wall, followed by a few seconds a large rolling boom of thunder echoing off the walls.

Ty tensed.

"Do you not like storms?"

"Why? Have you heard all soldiers' fear noise?"

"Are you okay?"

His chest inflated and deflated several times as he moved us toward the upholstered flower loveseat tucked under the windows. "Yesterday, I yelled at Trevor. The guy can't swing a hammer. He missed the nail and put a hole in the wall. Instead of taking responsibility or even apologizing, he accuses me of having PTSD. If I hadn't served in the military, then he would have never said that. I feel like everyone is always watching and judging me."

"The reason I asked is my mom hates storms. She'd never let me sit by the windows. I'd have to sit beside her in the bathtub and count the seconds between lightning flashes and thunder."

"Mabel, afraid of something? No way. You know I hate liars."

"If you want, I can call her to confirm, or—"

He pulled me close, his lips lowered to mine. "Or."

The night was perfect. And the only flaw was the sun rose, and I had to say goodbye. In the lobby, I lingered over a cup of coffee.

"You should take the day off." He reached over the table and tucked a few hairs behind my ears. "Please."

If I called in sick, I'd send an obvious message to Karen. Besides, I didn't own any shares in the company, and I wasn't an essential employee. But the churning in my stomach had me shaking my head. "I can't. The call center is short-staffed. If I don't show, then some poor worker won't get lunch or a bathroom break."

He arched his right eyebrow as his smile turned a bit toothy. "Can you at least be late to work?"

Anticipating his desire sent a shiver of delight up

my spine. With a quickening pulse, I thought of his arms wrapped around me and his sweet kisses on my neck. I nodded. His wanting me was more of a jolt than a double espresso.

An hour later, I glanced around the room as I slipped on my sandals. I stepped closer to Ty and rested both hands on his chest. "This was nice, but I enjoy spending time at the camper and cruising on the bike. I can't remember a summer when I have had more fun. Thank you."

"Me, too." He brushed a light kiss against my cheek. "I should let you go to work, but I'd rather rent the room for another night."

From somewhere, I gained the strength to step back. I gathered my things, and when I hoisted the backpack, I saw an envelope fluttered from the side pocket to the floor.

Ty scooped up the letter. He brushed a finger across the construction logo. "What's this?"

Shifting my gaze to the floor, I could feel guilt rumble in my stomach. I hadn't cheated on Ty; yet I couldn't look him in the eyes or shake the heat rising to my cheeks. Did I keep the letter because subconsciously, I wanted to believe JR wasn't guilty and a reasonable explanation existed? Or was I worried JR's words still had the power to sway me? Blindly, I reached for the letter and stuffed it into my purse. "Garbage. I've got to go." I rushed from the room, afraid I'd look up and see the same questions reflected in his gaze.

****

On Saturday, I walked into the apartment, set the motorcycle road test results on the coffee table, and headed to the bathroom.

When I shut the shower off, I heard a loud *rap-rap-rap*. After a hasty job drying off, I called out. "Just a minute." I slipped on shorts, tugged a tank top over my damp chest, and jogged through the living room, excited the backing material I ordered to finish Ty's quilt had arrived. I flung open the door. The person in the doorway wasn't the Speedy Delivery man. I opened and closed my mouth while widening my gaze.

"Wow, I hoped to surprise you, but I didn't think I'd shock you." Ty held out a bouquet of white daisies and pink carnations.

I stood immobile with my hair dripping on my shoulders.

"Sal, can I come in?" His hands brushed my shoulders. "Sal?"

"Yeah. Wow. I just got home and thought you were the delivery guy." I stepped aside, not knowing what else to do. Maybe he wouldn't notice the door to my craft room or see the quilt. One look at the fabric, and he'd know I was crafting him a bedcover.

He dropped the flowers onto the coffee table and wrapped both arms around me. "I missed you, Sal. It seems like months." His kisses quickly escalated from sweet to hungry.

I pulled him tighter, blinking to contain a surge of overwhelming emotion. He missed me.

"Did you miss me?" His lips brushed my forehead.

Not trusting myself to talk. I vigorously nodded.

"Why don't you finish getting dressed, and then you can show me the city?"

As much as I wanted to drag him into my bed, I didn't want him to notice the extra room or trust myself not to gush words of love. I rushed to the bathroom and pulled out the hairdryer. Five minutes later, I stepped out and saw Ty sitting with arms tightly crossed and frown lines wrinkling his forehead.

"Sal, is there something you want to say?"

I firmly planted both hands on my hips and shook my head.

"You passed your test." He pointed toward the coffee table.

"I know. Can you believe it?"

"Let's celebrate?"

"Definitely, but first, I need to swing by the No-Kill Shelter and drop off the quilt. The auction is tomorrow." I left Ty waiting by the door, as I rushed into the spare room and quickly returned with the quilt.

"Wow." He brushed a finger across the blue, yellow, and green material. "You did this? Where, how? Can I buy it?"

"If you think this is nice, you'll love my next quilted project. A traditional Log Cabin block pattern with warm, inviting autumn colors makes it the perfect blanket to wrap around your body on chilly nights. I also plan to embroider fabric hearts with Bernie, Wendy, or my dad's name."

His smile widened as his gaze softened. "You always surprise me."

"Today, it's you who shocked me. I'm glad you came." I drove to the shelter with Ty riding shotgun. Seeing him when I glanced to the right gave me goose bumps in a good way. After parking, I directed Ty through the entrance of the large converted warehouse.

Inside, dog barks and lonesome cries echoed off the cinder walls. Past the viewing and play area was another set of doors leading to the retail store and indoor kennels. The counter for adoptions, purchases, and donations was at the far end, with three lines of customers.

I chose the line with a young boy and watched him tug on a woman's hand.

The kid repeated in a sing-song way. "I want a big dog."

Ty nudged me. "Want to see if they have a shaggy, medium-sized?"

"You remembered." I softened my gaze…had he reconsidered leaving at the end of summer?

A slight bump on my right leg caught my attention. I glanced down before dropping to my knees.

A big, wet tongue brushed my cheek as his tail waved so hard his whole body shook. He was a bigger, shagger version of a Cairn Terrier.

I couldn't resist scratching under his chin.

The dog whined and tried to crawl into my arms.

Ty stooped and took the quilt from my arms.

I immediately bonded with this dog and sensed he liked me, too. He was the perfect size. Glancing up, I hoped to see a volunteer holding the other end of the leash and froze.

"Seems like Scruffy likes you. You've got good taste, boy, just like your owner. Sit." JR's voice vibrated the hairs on my arms.

I clenched my stomach and stood. He looked better than he had the last time I saw him. Gray streaked his dark hair. He had lost twenty pounds and maintained a tan. "Looks like prison life agreed with you." Feeling nothing but disdain, I shuffled forward a few feet and resisted the urge to gather the dog into my arms.

Paws rested again on my leg, and I reached for the furry head.

Ty wrapped an arm around my waist.

"So, this is what's gotten into you." JR's hand brushed my forearm.

Cringing, I yanked my arm away and heard the doggy growl.

"Sal, my gal, I understand you're upset with me, but I can't believe you were so disrespectful to my father. He employed you for over twenty years, and you couldn't even find the time to call him after he reached out. Despite that, I love you and always will."

The guilt over not dealing with the letter resurged as I watched Ty tighten his jaw. "If you haven't guessed, this is JR. Please don't shake his hand. You're liable to come back with only three fingers."

"Just so you know." JR smiled. "This guy doesn't love you. He'll break your heart. Call me when he does. Scooby and I will help you put the pieces back together again." He turned, dragging the dog behind him.

Scooby whined and spread his front legs but lost traction as JR yanked the leash and held out a large treat.

The dog glanced back before moving toward the biscuit.

Heaviness squeezed my heart. I took the quilt from Ty and dropped the bundle on the counter.

"Thank you, Sal." The volunteer carefully unfolded the quilt, her fingers running across the blue, green, and yellow triangles. "Is this the hidden star pattern? Oh my, this is gorgeous. This year, I have to win. The colors will go great in my bedroom."

I acknowledged her with a nod before turning and watching the shaggy dog disappear out the door with JR. I headed toward the door.

Ty tugged me to a stop. "Go ahead." He inclined his head toward the entrance. "I'll meet you in the car."

In the front seat, the temperature was close to a hundred degrees. I turned the air conditioning on high as I thought about the conversation with JR. Inside my purse, I found the rock with the word *believe* etched into the surface and traced the letters. Setting the rock aside, I dug to the bottom of the bag and found the crumbled construction envelope. With shaking fingers, I ripped open the flap and looked at the packet of papers. Skimming the cover letter, I shook my head, stuffed the contents into my purse, and turned on the radio. After the third song, I felt the pounding in my heart slow as I exhaled the anger. I had made a mistake dating JR, but I had done the right thing in seeing him jailed. The past slipped from my shoulders, and for the first time, I felt free to enjoy the moment and the day.

The door opened, and Ty slipped into the passenger seat.

I returned to the apartment, singing along slightly off-key to "Nobody But You" by Blake Shelton and Gwen Stefani. After exiting the car, I walked over to Ty and grabbed his hand. "Nobody…"

"You're in a good mood."

"I am now that you're here, and if you lend me money, then I'll buy lunch."

"Of course, lead the way."

Holding his hand, I walked through the complex, past the outdoor pool with the sounds of children squealing and the faint scents of chlorine and suntan lotions. "Did you bring a swimsuit?"

"I didn't even bring an overnight bag. I was driving to your mom's house, and instead of turning right, I took a left." He shrugged. "And I accidentally drove to your house."

The look in his eyes melted my heart. JR was wrong. Ty's love language differed from others. He didn't express his feelings verbally but with actions. I led him down the asphalt pedestrian path under the canopy of dense foliage, and immediately, the air felt cooler.

"This is nice. I wouldn't have expected to see so many trees in the city."

"The bike paths go for miles throughout the city. I thought about buying a bike but knew I wouldn't ride alone, so I bought a sewing machine, instead."

He slipped his hand from mine and wrapped his arms around me, dancing me to the path's edge. "It would be fun to rent some bikes." He leaned down and kissed me.

Excitement and pleasure made my skin tingle. Even though I didn't want to, I loved him with all my heart. Remembering his reaction when I quoted the lines from a song, I swallowed the sentiment and deepened the kiss, hoping he'd feel what I wouldn't say.

He grabbed my hand and tugged me forward. "So, is there someplace to eat around here? I skipped breakfast and lunch."

"This way." I led him down a path that wound through the quaint downtown, past coffee houses, and boutiques, before ending at the Depot Brewery. "They serve craft beers, awesome burgers, spicy tots, giant onion rings, and have outdoor seating."

The waitstaff showed us to a high table for two next to the split-rail fence that overlooked a grassy soccer field.

Moments later, the waitstaff returned with a peanut butter porter for Ty and a tart cherry sour for me.

Looking into my eyes, he lifted his dark beer. "To making a good choice."

I wrapped my hand around the cool glass but didn't hoist it. "Like?"

His smile turned crooked. "Taking a left instead of a right."

"A splendid choice." I lift my sour.

The glasses clinked.

But instead of taking a sip, he continued to hold the glass. "And…"

What was he wanting to say? Did he love me? Was he considering staying? I crossed my legs, wishing he'd finish his sentence. I was no longer breathing as I leaned over the table. "And?"

"You did it. You've got your endorsement." He grinned like he was the one who had won a gold medal.

Swallowing the beer with disappointment, I scooted back, studying his expression. Had I read him wrong? I was so sure he'd confess how he felt. I was certain he loved me. Maybe he was in denial.

"You don't look happy with the sour. Do you want me to order you something else?"

"No, the beer is delicious." I lifted the glass, and the intense cherry scent was followed by the tangy taste of acidic fruit with the slightest hint of sweetness. After another sip, I set the glass down and sighed.

"If it's not the beverage, is the problem with me?

Did I do something wrong?"

"I forgot to thank you for remodeling the house. Anything left to tackle?"

"Now that Travis has moved out, Trevor and I only have the bathroom and kitchen to paint before installing the floor coverings. I've been waiting for your mom to decide. She's always got an excuse not to go. So, on Tuesday, Amber and I will go."

I took a long sip, trying to ease the sudden tightness in my throat as I blinked back a tear. *I'm so tired of hearing that woman's name.*

He reached across the table and brushed his thumb against my hand. "What's wrong?"

Ty asking and not assuming he knew the answer made my love for him grow. But I felt foolish over my reaction to Amber. "Do you want me to be honest?"

"There are many things I can forgive, but dishonesty isn't one."

Instead of burying my concerns, I drew in a breath. "It bothers me you're going with Amber and that she was at the trailer. Could you go back to disliking her?" I watched him try to swallow the smile creasing his cheeks.

"It's important to talk about uncomfortable things. But there is no need to worry. I'm not interested in her. If I were, I wouldn't be here sitting with you."

I took a sip of my brew and knew I would remember the words long after he had returned to Wisconsin. Everything he did suggested his feelings were more than a summer fling. I could spend winters in my apartment and summers in the trailer.

The waitstaff approached the table with a tray and slid burgers, tots, and onion rings onto the table.

"Good choice." Ty grabbed his sandwich with both hands. Lettuce, tomato, sauce, and cheese oozed out the back of the bun as he bit down.

I slid napkins across the table and picked up my petite burger.

With only a few bites left, I pushed my plate to the center of the table and watched an older man walk past with a big lab. My concern for the dog in JR's possession immediately stifled my good mood. Was JR treating him well? Did he adopt a dog to lure me back? If only I had found the dog first...

Ty captured my hand and gave my fingers a reassuring squeeze. "I don't have to go with Amber, or is this something else—"

"The dog at the shelter. Did you see how hard he wagged his tail? He's everything I've wanted. I've imagined this moment for so long. And then I see the dog of my dreams is owned by JR. Sometimes, life doesn't seem fair."

"Life isn't. The first time I saw Amber, the past came flooding back, and I remembered my dad's frustration and disappointment. I didn't want any reminders of what a stupid kid I had been. But I am not the same person I was back then."

The waitstaff stopped next to the table.

Ty ordered another round.

I continued mulling over why he might have told me about Amber, then the second beer arrived. I took a sip, enjoying the sour, fruity taste, and caught Ty watching me. Something about how he held my gaze made me feel like we had known each other for a long time, like an old married couple. "Thanks for coming. I enjoy sitting and talking. Wait. Did you say Travis moved? Where? His girlfriend's?"

Laughter sputtered from Ty's lips as he shook his head. "About three conversations ago. He went to an extended stay motel."

"Did Mom make him leave?"

"No." His right eyebrow arched as his lips pursed. "She was disappointed by his decision." He ran his hand over the top of his head. "Your mom is impossible to figure out."

In the middle of a nod, I stopped. "Maybe she's lonely. I wonder if she should get a cat for a companion?"

"Something tells me your mom won't be lonely for long." Ty pushed the almost-full beer to the middle of the table.

I nodded and mimicked his actions. "Don't forget I'm buying. You can subtract the amount from the purchase price. We agreed on thirty thousand." I winked.

"Yep, twenty thousand."

After settling the tab, I strolled with Ty back through the downtown before taking the path back toward the apartment.

He squeezed my hand. "I can see why you like this area. With all the green space, I could almost forget I was in the city."

"And the location is so convenient. Even in the winter, they keep the path clear, and I can still walk for coffee or beer. It's beautiful. The trees are all covered in snow, my boots squeak against the cold pavement, and my breath comes out in white puffs. There is a quiet that I can't experience in any of the other seasons." I walked up the stairs and unlocked the door.

He followed. After stepping inside, he shut the door. "I'll have to take your word about the winter wonderland."

"Why?"

He lowered his mouth to mine, and the kiss went from sweet to hungry. His hands roamed over my body.

I pulled him closer, no longer thinking about anything other than the moment. I tugged him into the bedroom.

A few hours later, I stepped into the living room and found the sun was casting shadows. "A walk sounds like a perfect ending to the day." I stopped and picked the flowers up from the table. "But first, let me put these in water."

With his hand resting on my waist, I stepped into the kitchen and went to grab the vase from the cupboard. I heard the faucet turn on.

"Want a glass of water?"

"Nope."

He drank the water, set the glass on the counter, and entered the hall. "Hey, is that a second bedroom?"

"No." I dropped the flowers onto the counter and heard his footsteps continue.

"And is that another bathroom?"

I rushed toward the craft room, swiping my palms across my thighs, and abruptly stopped.

He stood blocking the doorway with his arms crossed firmly across his chest. "Is this a two-bedroom apartment?"

Why was he asking the question? He knew the answer. Refusing to be put on the defense after I had done nothing wrong, I met his gaze. "Why won't you be here to see the snow this winter? I could clean out the crafts—"

"Sal." He sighed, placing both hands on my shoulders. "You know I'm leaving. I never told you anything different." He nudged his head in the craft room direction. "I don't care that you didn't want your mom to live with you, but why lie? You could have told me about the little fib any time in the last couple of months." Creases deepened in his brow as his gaze turned weary, and his facial features softened. "Why hide things? I need to know you can talk to me."

How dare he make me the bad guy? I narrowed my gaze. "Don't twist this and make your lack of feelings and commitment my issue. You knew how I felt, yet you drove here and said all these sweet things. You make me think, maybe. Why?" I blinked rapidly, but still, a tear of frustration snuck down my cheek. "This thing between us seems special, and instead of hanging around for a few more months to see if anything develops, you're running away. And that's your secret power. Saying goodbye." I marched out of the kitchen, down the hall, and yanked the front door open.

He stood in the center of the living room, glaring. "I get it. You want me to leave? But instead of saying what's on your mind, you avoid issues—hiding behind your badge of fear. You ran from River City without a goodbye and didn't tell me JR sent you a letter or—"

White knuckling the doorknob I forced back tears of frustration. "Why do you care about who sends me letters? You're leaving. Would you feel better if I told you he still wanted to marry me, and his dad offered me eighty thousand dollars to manage the apartment complex he purchased? All I had to do was agree to hire JR. Happy?"

He widened his stance and held out his palms. "Sal, I don't want us to end like this—"

"Get out." I pointed a shaky finger at the open door. Adrenaline slammed my heart against my chest and vibrated the hairs on my arm. After seeing him clear the door, I refrained from slamming it shut, stumbled to the bed, and muffled my cries of frustration into the pillow.

Chapter Twelve

Twenty minutes later, I still couldn't find a comfortable spot on the bed, but at least my tears had stopped. I flopped onto my back, aimlessly scrolling through social media until I shut my eyes.

Buzz, buzz, buzz.

Disorientated, I switched on the bedside lamp. Blinking in the artificial light, I blindly reached toward the sound and found the phone under the bedspread.

Ty's name flashed.

Pain encased my heart. I stood and flung the device on the bed. If he wanted to leave, he could. But I also had choices, and I didn't want to hear any more of his flowery words. He's the coward running away. Let him chase across the country. He'll figure out life isn't about where you've been but the people who shared your journey.

The buzzing stopped and then started.

Rushing down the hall, I placed my hands over my ears to muffle the sound. *One more call, and I am shutting the phone off.* I flicked the kitchen light switch, and the first thing I spotted was the lifeless flowers. I scooped the droopy blossoms and watched a card flutter to the counter. Curling my lip, I sneered. "No flowery words or poetic sentiment will change things." I chopped a few inches off the stems and arranged the white daisies and pink carnations. They still looked sad and wilted. What they needed was an aspirin. In the bedroom, I searched the nightstand drawers and found hand sanitizer and cough drops, but no aspirin.

The sound of the phone buzzing captured my attention.

I sighed—four missed calls from Ty, two from an unknown number, and one voice message. Against my better judgment, I played the recording.

"Sal, it's Ty. Your mom fell, and I called an ambulance. She's at the hospital. Call me."

Clutching the phone tighter, I redialed.

After three rings, Ty answered.

"Is she going to be okay?"

"The nurse claims she can't tell me anything because I'm not family. Something about patient rights. I told them to call you."

"Okay. If you see Mom, tell her I'm on my way." I ended the call, slipped into yoga pants and a T-shirt, and tossed some clothes into my backpack.

In my car, I called Ty again. "What hospital?"

"Regional. Are you okay driving?"

"Yeah, fine." I disconnected, eager to get on the road. Well after midnight, I pulled into the parking ramp and hurried through the emergency doors to the information desk. "My mom, Mrs. Ridel, arrived by ambulance hours ago. Can I see her? Is she okay?" Fear and uncertainty tightened my throat. I fumbled through my purse, found my driver's license, and slid the card under the glass enclosure.

The woman behind the partition jotted down my information and gave instructions to sit in the waiting room, and she'd find someone to provide an update.

Not wanting to make small talk with anyone in the

waiting room, I moved to the back corner, seeing a row of three unoccupied chairs. Chills knocked my knees together. I pulled my arms tighter across my chest. Was she dead? I heard footsteps and looked up, expecting to see someone from the hospital staff.

Ty stepped closer. "Hey." He held out a steamy cup.

I reached out my hand, wishing he'd gather me into his arms and whisper *everything would be okay.* But instead, I watched him place the coffee in my outstretched fingers.

"You going to be okay?"

Pretending to take a sip, I nodded.

"The ambulance attendants asked about insurance and medicines. Before driving here, I sorted through the medicine cabinet. Quite a few bottles had my dad's name. I stuffed them all in the purse. They said someone would be out for it, but that was two hours ago." He dangled the bright-orange pocketbook in front of me.

I set the cup on the table and reached for her oversized bag, smiling at her peculiar scent of lavender, vanilla, and coffee as memories of her smile flashed through my thoughts.

"It's been hours, and I'm not even sure if a doctor has seen her yet."

Clutching the purse tighter, I drew in a breath, feeling overwhelmed by a multitude of emotions. "Do you think—" The sounds stuck in my throat. I swallowed. "You saw her. Is she going to—?"

"The paramedics took her vitals. Everything looked good." He rested a hand on my trembling knee. "They thought a concussion, possibly a broken hip, but no mention of heart attack or stroke."

I noticed the worry lines etched into his face and wanted to comfort him, but the effort needed to move was too great.

He removed his hand.

A chill replaced the warmth from his touch. I already missed him. "Thanks for being here and calling me. You don't have to stay." I hugged Mom's purse to prevent my arms from going around him.

"You sure?" He stuffed his hands into his pockets, shifting his weight, as his gaze lingered.

Knowing he wouldn't be around for the rest of my life toughened my resolve. I had to start living without him. I nodded and watched him walk away without saying goodbye. He didn't even ask me to call him with updates. I picked up my coffee cup. I'll never feel the warmth of his touch or dance across the room gazing into his eyes...I blinked, refusing to let any tears fall.

An hour later, a nurse came and explained the situation.

Ty had been right—concussion and fractured hip. Mom was in surgery.

The nurse instructed me to the family room and told me someone would come and get me when Mabel was out of recovery.

Three hours later, I had her room number. Taking baby steps and holding my breath, I walked in and saw her lifeless body on the bed. If not for seeing the slight movement in her chest and the machine flashing her vitals, I would have thought she was dead.

The doctor was tall with a thick head of white hair and looked like he had never smiled. He introduced himself and then used his hands to explain where the break occurred and what he did to repair the hip. "She'll be asleep for at least a couple of hours. I'll keep her for three days, and if everything looks good, she will be discharged."

I sighed. "That's good news. She'll be glad to get home."

"Do you live with her? Or will someone else be managing her care?" He pulled a tablet from his white lab coat and started typing.

"She lives alone. Will that be a problem?"

He stopped keying, and his gaze bore through me. "If you or someone else won't be available to assist her, then she'll be discharged to a transitional care unit or a nursing home until she can live independent." He turned and walked out.

I pushed away the guilt from not offering to be Mom's caregiver. I had never changed a bandage or taken care of a broken bone. Besides, she'd only need to stay in a facility for a few days.

****

At Mom's house, I cringed at the sight of Ty's truck. Why did he have to be here? A huff of air escaped from my lungs. The sun was overhead as I walked up the front steps, holding my backpack and the orange-and-yellow-flowered purse. Tilting my chin, I moved through the door.

Inside, I heard noises coming from the bathroom. I set everything down in the entryway and headed down the hall.

Ty glanced up as he crawled on the floor, pushing a rag. "How's your mom?"

"They did surgery to repair her broken hip, and she has some stitches on her forehead but no brain swelling.

They'll release her to a transitional care place in three days, and then they release her back home when she's ready."

"Mabel's okay with the nursing facility?"

"She's still medicated, so I haven't talked to her."

He dipped a towel into the bucket.

"What are you doing?"

"I thought I'd clean up the mess."

Lack of sleep had dulled my senses as I puzzled over the situation. "She fell in the bathroom?"

"Must have slipped on water when getting out of the tub."

"Oh." I covered my open mouth as I tried to shake the visual of Ty finding my mom naked. "I'm so sorry. I can't even imagine. How did they get her into the stretcher without clothes?"

"I grabbed one of my dad's old T-shirts and pulled it over her head before the ambulance arrived. As the attendants wheeled her out the front door, she cussed because the front of her shirt had *Old Guys Rule* printed in big letters."

"Again, I'm so sorry." What would have happened if he hadn't come by? She could have bled out on the floor. Fending off a sudden chill, I wrapped my arms around my stomach and leaned against the door frame.

He held my gaze. "Sal, it's okay. She's going to be fine."

I slumped to the hardwood, regretting the words I spewed. He's been honest and kind. Did he regret getting upset? I couldn't read his expression. He wasn't smiling or scowling. Was he disappointed?

He rested a hand on my shoulder. "Your mom and I chatted while waiting for the ambulance. She was very adamant about not going to a nursing home."

So many things I wanted to say ran through my mind, but the words didn't come. What if she refused to go to a transitional care facility? How much time could I afford to take off work?

"Sal, will you be okay?"

I cocked my head at the huskiness in his voice as tears stung my eyes. Not trusting myself to speak, I nodded my response.

"Call me if you need anything."

Sitting on the floor, I heard the front door open and close. Twenty minutes later, I went to put my stuff in the spare bedroom and found the furniture under plastic in the middle of the room. With no choice, I moved into Mom's room, plopping onto the bed, left a voice mail for Karen, and texted Joe and Lisa. Hugging myself I drifted to sleep. I opened my eyes, to see shadows dancing across the floor. With a racing heart, I grabbed for my phone. *How long had I been asleep?* I cringed, *after five.* I skipped showering and rushed back to the hospital.

Mom sat in bed, glaring. "About time. A doctor tried to tell me I'd be going to a care facility. Shoot me now because I won't go."

I inched forward, happy to see her back to her old self. "How do you feel?"

"My hip is on fire, and I can't get out of bed. What am I, five? Get me out of here."

"You just had surgery. You'll be in the hospital for three days. I'll let your friends know, and they can come visit."

"No." She shook her fist. "I will not let people see me looking like an invalid. Don't tell anyone."

"River City isn't that big. Besides, they're all at the age when falls happen."

"Not to me, I'm spry and in good health. The issue was the bath mat. I stepped out of the tub, and the rug shot out from under my feet like a toboggan down an icy hill." Mom pointed. "Where is he? Did you make up yet?"

I shrugged. Had Ty blabbed about our fight? "Did you hear I passed my motorcycle test?"

"Bernie was right." She grinned. "Knew you had gumption, said as much after watching you testify in court. He told me you were made of sturdy stuff, and the motorcycle would remind you. I'm so proud. You should keep the bike."

"You'll need the money."

She shook her head. "I've got money stashed."

"What?" I narrowed my gaze. "I know you always worked, but I thought you were broke."

She scuffed. "You and the rest of the world."

I crossed my arms. "Well, I'm nearly destitute, so I'll keep Ty's money. Has the apartment contacted you about when they might have availability?"

"Oh yeah, I can move in anytime. I already paid the deposit and the first month's rent."

I shook my arms above my head and stomped closer to the bed. "What?"

"Bernie and I had already talked about moving when he got the diagnosis. He knew he had little time, so we devised a plan. Worked perfectly, the boys got the summer to bond, and you got your spark back and a little bonus action."

"You two planned and orchestrated all this? Was a broken hip part of the scenario?"

"Of course not. But if my fall brings you and Ty to your senses…nope, not even that is worth the pain and humiliation of lying in a hospital bed." She grabbed my hand. "Ty's a good guy. I know you don't *need* a man, but sometimes life is fun with one."

I curled my lip. "Yeah, he's great, and he's leaving."

"And you're mad because you want him to stay?"

"That and I ran into JR, and he had the dog I always talked about getting. Fluffy, sweet, and he loved me."

"JR? What a waste of a man, why wouldn't he—"

"The dog loved me. I could tell. He licked my leg and face. I always wanted a dog and a home."

Mom crooked her finger and motioned me closer.

I leaned forward.

She socked me in the arm.

"What was that for?"

"You don't need to act like a victim. Get the dog, the man, whatever you want. Life is short. Don't wait for tomorrow."

"I know, but the dog will die, the man will leave, and the—"

"Ask yourself."

I cringed. If she said anything about being in a nursing home, then I'd punch her back.

"Sally! Pay attention. I don't want to repeat myself. Ask yourself, is being in love and saying goodbye better than never falling in love?" She didn't wait for a reply and motioned toward the door.

If she had asked a week ago, I would have said *yes, love was worth the cost*, but now wallowing in the constant pain of knowing I'll never feel his arms around me or hear his voice whisper in my ear, I wasn't sure... I stepped into the hall.

"Sal, bring me back something suitable to wear."

I left the hospital and drove to Ty's trailer to thank him again for cleaning up and caring for things. As I punched in the code, I puzzled over the fact most of the campers were dark, and I hadn't seen one campfire. Then I remembered today was Sunday. When I got to Ty's trailer beside his truck, I saw a ruby-red sports car with vanity plates *Amber No.1*. I slouched in my seat as I drove past, grateful they weren't outside.

However, at the next site, I spotted Wayne and Barb standing next to their vehicle, waving. But I couldn't stop and pretended not to see them. I took a left and followed the loop to the exit. Not wanting to go home, I checked the time. Hopefully, the ice cream shop didn't close before nine.

I parked at River Park and walked to Sweets, ordering a double scoop, chocolate chunk and salted caramel in a waffle cone. I inhaled the scent of sugar and vanilla coming from the waffle makers. As I strolled next to the river, I couldn't help but remember my walks with Ty. If only I could have embraced the notion of a summer fling. Was Amber good at saying goodbye? I took a large bite and grimaced—brain freeze. After stuffing the last bit of waffle cone into my mouth, I returned to my car. I couldn't change my past, but could I change the future?

Chapter Thirteen

On Monday, I stopped by the hospital with a bag of Mom's things, and as soon as I stepped into the room, I saw fireworks.

"Sal, tell her." Mom sat on the edge of the bed and pointed. "I am not going to a nursing home. My daughter will bring me home. She'll stay with me."

A woman held out her right hand. "Hello, I'm Lynn, the occupational therapist. Mabel, can your daughter watch while you work on your transfers?"

Mom clutched the walker in front of her. "You can invite the entire hospital. I don't care. Just get me out of here. I want to go home."

I stood against the wall and watched Mom grimace as she followed instructions on how to get out of bed.

The therapist asked a lot of questions about the height of the bed at home, if I had grab bars in the bathroom, and a tub chair for transfers.

The thought of Mom using assistive devices was at odds with how I perceived her. She was strong and fiercely independent. I glanced over and saw the sweat on Mom's brow but also determination in her gaze and knew I, too, was made of stronger stuff, and I'd manage the long list of things.

She handed me a list of equipment and left.

I stayed until Mom started snoring. All the way home, I couldn't stop thinking of Ty and Amber and

Scruffy Dog with JR. Everyone had a happy ending but me. Stepping into the kitchen, I could tell someone had been in the house because the table was full of tarps, brushes, rollers, trays, and three paint cans. By the time I had dragged the painting supplies to the spare bedroom, sweat soaked my shirt.

I opened the windows but got no relief. The outside air didn't feel any cooler. With earbuds in, I popped the top off the can and dipped the roller into the tray. Something about covering up the old dingy green paint that had been behind the wallpaper with the clean, crisp white linen was satisfying. As I jammed to songs from the nineties, I could feel my spirits improve. All I needed now was a fresh hair color and a makeover.

Old Man Sumpter's job offer about managing his apartment building got me thinking. Showing apartments, handling rentals, scheduling maintenance, and planning events to grow the community, I could do those things. Now, all I needed was time to research and update my resume. I couldn't hear the growl of my gut, but I could feel the hunger pang. But I didn't stop until I finished the last wall. With the roller in my hand, I stepped back to see if I had missed any spots and bumped into a warm body. Terror racked my body. I screamed.

Hands gripped my shoulders.

"It's okay. Turn down your music or take out your headphones."

I didn't have to turn to know who had grabbed me, but I did.

Ty stood in a crisp green polo shirt and tan shorts.

I looked past him and fixed my gaze on the woman behind him. Gorgeous with a vibrant smile, long curled hair, and artfully applied makeup. I knew she was older than me, but I wouldn't have guessed.

"Sal, meet Amber. She's our real estate agent."

After glancing at the paint-laden roller in my right hand and the splats on my clothes, I smirked. "I'd offer my hand, but it's covered in linen white." I chuckled, masking the anger in my voice. "Guess you forgot to mention you were coming over. Last I heard, you were shopping on Tuesday."

"I am, but Amber wanted to stop by today and look at the house. Is that okay?"

"It's your house, not mine. I'll head back to the cities on Wednesday." I wondered when he'd ask if I made an appointment with the attorney.

He widened his stance. "I guess you'll be taking your mom with you."

"No, Mom will live here, or—" I stopped from saying her apartment. He didn't need to know she had a place. I set the roller down in the pan, spotted Amber's hand on his forearm, stooped, picked up the paint lid, and pounded the top back onto the can more forcefully than necessary.

"You can't leave your mom here. She's going to need help. I've got plans, but—"

"Nice to meet you, Amber." I shifted my weight, grabbed the tray with the roller, stood, and stepped toward the doorway.

"I love the paint colors." Amber brushed against Ty. "Will you complete the painting by Wednesday?"

"I'm not sure, but I'm certain Ty will keep you informed on my progress." Making direct eye contact with Ty, I took another step.

He turned and motioned for Amber to move.

Did he notice more things were changing than the color of the walls? I no longer wore my fear, and if he wasn't careful, then I would drench him in the paint like my mom had peppered him with ice cream. I headed to the utility sink in the laundry area, and instead of wrapping my hands around Ty, I squeezed the roller until the water ran clear.

When I checked the clock, I picked up the pace. The staff would have already brought Mom her dinner. I rushed to the car, not even bothering to brush my hair or check for paint splatter on my face. At the hospital, I faked a smile as I stepped into the room.

Mom crossed her arms and glared. "Where have you been?"

"Painting, and Ty showed up with the real estate woman."

Her frown turned into a giant smile. "Amber. Isn't she nice? She's a real looker, with lots of sales and awards. She does better than the men in her office."

"And now she's probably wearing the Miss Wisconsin crown." I clenched my hands.

"Looks like you didn't patch things up with Ty. That's too bad. But, at least, you had a little fun."

Was Mom making me feel better with humor, or was she trivializing my feelings? I clenched my hands. If she equated this to puppy love, I'd have a meltdown. With my emotions ricocheting, I searched for a safe topic. "Hey, how'd therapy go?"

"Hip hurts like hell, but they tell me tomorrow will be easier." Mom crooked her finger and motioned me closer.

I leaned over the bed.

She spoke in such hushed tones.

189

And I had to ask her to repeat herself twice.

"I'm not going to a skilled nursing facility. Tell them you'll take me home, and when I'm in the house, you can return to Minneapolis. I'll be fine. No one will know."

As I recalled the blood on the bathroom floor, I swallowed the metallic taste in my mouth, What if Ty hadn't been there? "No. The doctor was adamant someone needed to be home."

"They have to say that because they don't want to take any responsibility."

"How about you go to the care facility for just two days? I'll come back on Saturday and bring you home."

She shook her fist. "Sal, I'm the only family you got, and if you send me to the nursing home, then that will be the last time you'll see me."

This time, I wouldn't let her browbeat me into submission. "It will only be for a few days. When I drive back next weekend, I can help you furnish your apartment."

"I might only be there for a few days, but they will be my first few days of never having a daughter. You'll be as dead to me as Bernie."

Her doctors and therapists were in River City, and leaving her at my apartment while I worked wouldn't be any better than leaving her home alone. I rubbed my temples. "Okay. I'll work out something."

****

The next day, I awoke to the smell of coffee, but instead of rushing from the bed, I pulled the covers over my head. I'd rather die of heat and dehydration than face Ty. Tension clenched every muscle in my body. I strained my ears. Did he bring Ms. Wisconsin with him? Clutching hands, I flew from the bed, stomping down the hallway. How dare he bring Amber back to the house? I'd be leaving in a few days. Couldn't he wait? Wearing only a nightshirt, I stormed through the doorway and scanned the area for Amber. Unclenching my fist, I narrowed my gaze on Ty. "Come to check on my painting progress. You can tell the new Ms. Wisconsin that I won't finish on Wednesday."

He rolled his eyes, exhaling through flared nostrils.

"Oh, yeah. I forgot you're all about honesty. I drove by the trailer Sunday night, hoping to talk, but you had company."

"Amber stopped by."

"Are you sleeping with her? I saw her car."

"You jealous?"

I crossed my arms across my chest and felt the nightshirt shift higher.

His gaze drifted lower, his blue eyes darkened, and his hand tentatively reached forward before dropping to his side.

"You're not answering the question."

"No, she's not you. There's coffee and some breakfast sandwiches on the counter." He brushed past.

A moment later, the sound of the front door closing echoed through my heart. Cupping the hot brew, I pushed aside the conversation, focusing on what I needed to do. I called into work, hoping to hear Karen's prerecorded message.

"Sally, I'm so glad you called..."

The sensation of a hundred ants marching up my forearms had me reaching for the kitchen chair as I tried to focus.

"You're eligible for twelve weeks of family leave,

but unfortunately, the new law offering compensation doesn't go into effect until January one of twenty twenty-six..."

I sat staring out the window until I heard her ask for how long I planned to be gone? I clenched my jaw. She didn't once ask how my mother was doing or how I was coping. After assuring her I'd get back, I disconnected.

With no outlet for my energy, I checked the bedroom to see if the walls needed another coat, but everything looked good, so I headed to the bathroom. When lunchtime rolled around, the bathroom was a sunny yellow. The spare bedroom and Mom's bed had clean sheets, and a path was cleared to the kitchen and bathroom for the walker.

By three o'clock, I had bought everything on the equipment list the occupational therapist suggested. But when I started the installation, I realized Ty's toolbox was no longer in the kitchen. After searching the house, I gave up and grabbed a knife from the butcher block to tighten the Phillip screws. Draped over the toilet, I had already attached the riser and was working on a grab bar. I had one screw left.

The phone rang and vibrated across the plastic bath chair.

Pounding on the front door echoed.

I jerked—a searing pain shot through my left hand. Cringing, I glance down at the tip of the steak knife buried into my left palm. Blood spurted onto the freshly painted walls.

Frustration had me swearing. I yanked the knife free and placed my hand under running water. I slumped against the sink. Instead of watching pink-tinged water swirl down the drain, I started a mental list…find bandages, clean up, and toss the knife into the trash.

The sound of the front door closing sent an unpleasant shiver down my spine as footsteps stopped at the entrance to the bathroom. I didn't bother to turn around. I knew Ty stood there.

"What did you do?"

"Someone took their toolbox, and I needed a screwdriver. If you had walked in like you normally—"

"Let me see." He wrapped his hand around my wrist, pulling my hand out from beneath the running water. After a glance, he shoved the gaping wound back under the cold tap.

The front door slammed again.

My phone chirped—a voice mail.

With one hand, I listened to the message.

"Sal, come get me. I checked myself out, and I'm in the lobby."

I turned the water off with my elbow, wrapped a towel around my hand, and sidestepped Ty in the hallway.

"Come on." He nodded toward the bathroom. "I'll bandage your hand."

"I need to pick up my mom. She's checked out of the hospital and could call a taxi." I tried calling Mom, but she didn't answer, so I left a message for her to wait. Visions of riding around River City popped into my head. Who knows where she'd end up? I reached for my purse.

Ty blocked the path. "It'll only take a minute. Besides, you need both hands to get your mom into the car."

"Fine, but be quick." I snorted through my nostrils like a racehorse.

He removed the blood-soaked towel and attached adhesive strips to close the wound.

Watching him work, I remembered the kisses. As soon as I saw him smooth the last piece of the bandage, I rushed out of the house, stopping at the driver's door of my car. *Keys.* With no choice, I re-entered the house, pushing empty equipment boxes aside, trying to remember when I had last seen them.

A jingle caught my attention.

Ty stood in the kitchen doorway, holding my key ring. "Looking for these? Why don't you let me drive?"

"Fine, but only because I'll need two people to wrestle her into the car." Feeling agitated and confused, I reminded him to grab the walker. Why did the sight of him cause my emotions to roller-coaster? I want to pull him close, feel his lips on mine, and punish him for leaving me. Would I regret watching him drive away without telling him how much I'd miss our time together?

Chapter Fourteen

Late Tuesday evening, Mom winced and cussed as she transferred out of the car and required lots of assistance and encouragement to manage the stairs into the house. "I'm going to lie down for a minute, and I don't need any help." The walker banged across the floor and into a doorframe.

After exchanging glances with Ty, I stepped into the kitchen and leaned against the counter.

He pulled out a chair and sat. "I ordered the flooring, and the installation is scheduled for two weeks from today."

I wanted to ask if he'd still be here when the materials arrived and what he meant about Amber not being me.

"Will you be here tomorrow?" He stood and took a step closer.

"I called requested family leave, and of course, Karen couldn't wait to tell me the time off would be without pay. I'm going to need the proceeds from the bike sale.

"If you're asking if I still want to buy the bike, the answer is *yes*." He ran a hand across his chin. "Twenty thousand, right?"

Is he renegotiating now that I'm desperate? Drawing a deep breath, I widened my stance, glanced over, and caught his wink. "Ha, ha. You know it's twenty-eight, minus the lessons and accessories." I reached out and playfully brushed my hand across his stomach. I widened my gaze, knowing I no longer had the right to touch him. But instead of finding reproach reflected in his gaze, I watched him grin.

"Don't forget about the cost of lunch. That was a good burger. I sure could go for one now. I'm starved."

"Me, too."

"Would you settle for a pizza delivered?"

"Of course." I watched him order an extra-large with the works and a six-pack of beer. While I waited, I helped him move all the paint supplies to the basement. As I wiped the table, I heard the walker hitting the wall and glanced at Mom. "Remember, stand up straight and stay within the frame of the walker."

She snarled, scratched her bottom, and groaned. "I'm starved." She ran the walker into the table. "Got anything to eat."

"I'm headed to the door. We've got pizza coming." Ty winked.

After getting her settled on a cushion, Ty placed the pizza on the center of the table, leaving barely enough room for our plates.

Mom grabbed a slice with toppings and cheese dripping from the edges and bit into the pizza with gusto.

Ty rushed to get napkins and glasses in place. "Want a beer?" He set a can of hazy IPA in front of her.

Shaking my head, I reached for Mom's beer. "She'll have water or milk. She already got enough drugs in her system."

"More for us." He laughed and filled a glass with water.

For once, Mom didn't comment. She kept chewing.

After my first bite, I understood. The mozzarella cheese was thick and toasted, the tomato sauce was tangy, and the sausage had hints of fennel seeds. I ate two slices in silence before leaning back and enjoying the hoppy taste of the beer as the conversation evolved around the weather and the house.

Twenty minutes later, Mom closed her eyes.

I rose and reached for her walker. "Come on, sleepyhead, time for bed."

Ty stood. "I'll clean up."

Thirty minutes later, I entered the spotless kitchen and found Ty sitting at the table, scrolling. "I thought you'd be gone."

"Yeah, I wasn't sure." He rubbed his hand across the stubble on his chin. "Disappointed?"

Surprised and slightly comforted by his reaction...knowing he was as unsure and fumbling through this new us gave me strength. "No." I pulled out a chair and sat. "I'm going to miss you." I told him about updating my resume and how I planned on looking at shelters for a dog.

He told me about moving Travis back to his girlfriend's house, how he and Trevor played miniature golf, and the three of them were meeting for breakfast in the morning.

After agreeing to another beer, I hoisted my glass. "To meddling parents and their good sense."

"Huh?" He arched his right eyebrow.

"Mom and Bernie had already planned on moving to an apartment when he received the cancer diagnosis. So, then they changed their plans and the will, hoping you and your brothers would bond over the remodeling project…at first, I was miffed, but then I realized I wouldn't have had the opportunity to get to know you." I tapped his glass.

He returned the clink. "To them, to us, to some memorable nights I'll never regret." After talking for another hour, he left without a kiss goodbye.

I was glad. I didn't want a peck goodbye, I wanted a goodnight kiss.

Thursday morning, I once more awoke to the smell of coffee. But this time, I stopped at the bathroom, combed my hair, and brushed my teeth before stepping into the kitchen wearing the cute cherry summer pajamas Wendy bought.

"Morning, gorgeous." Ty stepped forward with a cup of coffee.

I accepted the cup, but instead of taking a sip, I brushed a slight kiss on the side of his face. "Thanks."

A slight blush tinged his cheeks. "I'll be back after breakfast." He grinned and walked backwards out the door.

After breakfast, I woke up Mom. She was tired, and after assisting her to the bathroom, she demanded to be put back in bed. I propped pillows behind her and turned on the TV.

Sometime after ten, Ty stopped by.

I helped him paint the kitchen. When I woke Mom in the evening, the place looked fresh and clean.

For dinner, Ty ordered fried chicken, coleslaw, and potato salad.

The two of us ate while Mom pushed food around her plate and entertained us with stories about club members.

"Sounds more like a sitcom on TV than real life." I

lifted a can of tropical IPA.

"Honest." She held up her hand.

"So, Mabel, do you have advice or words of wisdom for me now that I'm retired? Have any regrets I shouldn't repeat." He lifted a can of hazy IPA. "Like don't drink from a can."

"First thing, never refuse drugs. Whatever they're giving me is good. The only time I felt better was with Bernie." She batted her eyelashes as a slight pink tinged crept across her cheeks. "I regret not marrying your dad."

"Why?" I took another sip of beer and let the cool, hoppy taste ease my tension.

"Marriage meant nothing to me, but having the ceremony was important to Bernie. He wanted to call me his bride and never had the chance." She pushed the half-eaten chicken aside. "I need to rest."

This time, I didn't follow her. I felt she wasn't looking for company. The sound of a walker pushing the bedroom door closed punctuated the silent air.

Ty covered his face with both hands. "How could I be so insensitive?"

Giving his hand a reassuring squeeze, I waited until he uncovered his face. "Remember when you asked why I didn't ask my mom about my dad? Sometimes, the answer isn't worth the pain the question caused, but the hard part is I never knew if the subject was off-limits until she responded. Tomorrow, she will wake up, and you'll again be her favorite, even though she'll never tell you." I stood, grabbed two beers from the refrigerator, and nodded toward the front step. "Come on."

I sat next to Ty on the front steps. After several

minutes of staring at the street, I took a deep breath, leaned over, and kissed him. Tonight, I didn't want to think about earlier conversations or his leaving.

He rested his hands on my shoulders and ended the kiss. "Sal, I'm leaving in a few weeks."

Looking into his baby-blue eyes, I nodded. "I know, and I don't want to rehash things, but I want to thank you for being here and helping."

He slid an arm around my shoulders and pulled me closer. "I'm glad I could be here for you. We're family and almost stepsiblings."

"Eww." I tried to push him away. "Mood wrecker, why would you say that?"

He tightened his grip. "Sal, some conversations are awkward, but that doesn't mean we shouldn't have them. Let's laugh and tell people our family tree has no branches."

"Let's say you picked me up at a bar." Instead of scooting away from him, I laid my head on his shoulder. "Wait, why are we having this conversation? Are you planning on inviting me to a year-end party at the campground?"

"Or…"

He didn't finish the sentence. Instead, his lips found mine.

Then the mosquitoes discovered me. I rushed back inside, slapping at the tiny, blood-sucking monsters. "Well, I'm telling people we met on the dance floor. You have all the moves."

With most of the living room covered in plastic, the only place to hang out was the kitchen or spare bedroom. After checking on Mom, the two of us danced down the hallway, and after three twirls and a dip, I reached the bedroom.

He spun me away and put his hips in motion. "But my best move is the back rub."

Laughing, I rushed back into his arms. "Definitely could use one after all the painting."

The following day, after a shower and bandage change, I helped Mom get her clothes from the bottom dresser and left to make breakfast. In the kitchen, Ty greeted me with a kiss and a coffee.

As I made omelets, the two of us talked about Mom, the weather, and the house.

At the first sound of the walker, Ty jumped. "Should I slip out the back door?"

"I broke my hip, not my hearing. Of course, you can stay. I've got therapy at ten. Someone needs to buy me a cane?"

After placing a cushion on the kitchen chair, I watched her wince as she sat.

"I planned to buy one in a few weeks—"

"Nope, today or tomorrow, I'm graduating to the cane. This stupid thing doesn't even fit in the bathroom, and I put a gouge on the hall wall." She took a bite of the egg.

Ty added milk, sugar, and vanilla to the coffee before setting the cup before her. "I can go out and get one."

She smiled. "You were always the smart one. You know exactly how I like my coffee and what to say. When you get the cane, try to find something fitting."

"Sure thing." He grinned.

By the time Mom finished breakfast, fatigue etched her face. After getting her comfortable in bed, I returned to Ty.

"Stubborn as they get. That's what my dad said about her, and then he'd add he wouldn't want her any other way." He wrapped an arm around me. "There is an hour before the therapist comes." He wiggled his eyebrows. "Need a back rub?"

Standing in the kitchen, with the sunshine through the window, I knew I'd have to come to terms with his leaving, but I also knew I could put it off for one more hour.

"This fall—"

"Shhhh." I clamped a hand over his mouth.

"Sal—"

I removed my hand and tried silencing him with a kiss.

He gripped my shoulders and held me at arm's length. "This fall. Come with me."

"What?" I searched his eyes. "You mean…Oh, oh." Everything tingled. I felt lightheaded and charged. I hopped like a child's wind-up toy before answering him with kisses.

With Mom's snores echoing in the hallway, I rushed with him to the spare room.

****

The following five days went by in a blur. So many last-minute things needed finishing, and when I thought I had everything done, I'd find three more things to add to the list.

Mom started walking with a cane, and in a few more weeks, she'd be driving.

One day, I took a break from the house and drove Mom to the new downtown apartment. On her seventh floor balcony, I stood enjoying her view of the bluffs, but with no place to sit, she grew restless.

She rubbed her hip. "I need furniture and something besides painted walls to stare at…want to drive me to The Club? I'd like to attend the monthly meeting." After receiving agreement, she asked if I'd snap a picture of her by the window so she could show everyone her view.

I shook my head at her outrageous poses and facial features, knowing I'd share a few shots with Joe and Lisa.

On Thursday, I waved goodbye. Part of me thought driving back to the city for one day was a waste of time, but Mom didn't need me, and I was running out of money.

Instead of feeling a sense of welcome when I entered my apartment, I was overcome with loneliness until I spotted the quilt I'd started for Ty. Even if I worked all night, I couldn't get the bedcover done, but after tossing in a load of laundry, I busied myself with adding the last few rows of patches. At midnight, I shut off the machine after hearing the neighbor pound on my ceiling. In bed, I listened to people walking down the hallway, the traffic on the freeway, and the distant sounds of ambulances. After living with the noise for many years, I wondered why everything sounded so loud.

With the pillow on top of my ears, I tried to sleep. The thought of traveling with Ty in the fall vanished as reality replaced the images of mountains, toes dipping into the Pacific, and gazing at the tall redwood trees. With my meager savings, I couldn't pay for my apartment without working. The plans I made with Ty dissipated like steam from a kettle. Office managers rarely worked remotely. I'd be without a job, and I needed medical insurance. The only reasonable solution would be to say goodbye to Ty at the end of summer.

Not looking forward to a day with Karen, I tossed on jeans and a T-shirt and packed a hasty lunch. Outside, the rain pounded the pavement and soaked my jacket. The wet, dark day matched my mood. Thirty minutes later, I sloshed into work. I hung up my jacket and hoped the sleeves would be dry by the time I left work.

"So." Joe rushed over. "How's Mom? And are you wearing a glow?"

"She's doing better. The doctor figures she should be fit to drive in two weeks, and by then, she'll have everything moved to the new apartment." I wrinkled my nose. "Is that coffee?"

"Yeah, but first, the important stuff. Is Ty moving into your place, or will you look for a bigger apartment?"

"Caffeine before answers." Stepping into the lunchroom, I widened my gaze, pointing at a new coffee machine dispensing individual cups, a fruit basket, and a box of bakery goods. "What's this?"

"You missed all the excitement. The service technicians met with Mr. Smith on Tuesday and presented their case. On Wednesday, the owners announced there would be changes. A two percent raise across the board, new coffee machines installed, and the feasibility study was in the trash."

"How did Karen take the news?"

"I'm guessing she wasn't very receptive because they posted her position. Lisa and I think you should apply. You'd be great."

Lisa bustled into the space, grinning, with flushed

cheeks.

While waiting for my cup, I glanced again at Lisa. "You didn't get a haircut or color, but you look different? Did you always wear glasses?"

Joe swished his hands like a window washer. "Lisa has a mystery man."

She giggled, looking ten years younger.

Whatever put the glow on her cheeks, I hoped the newfound joy would last.

Joe jabbed me. "Is Ty going to leave?"

Carrying a banana and steamy coffee, I nodded and headed to my workstation. I was a little surprised Joe or Lisa hadn't followed. Apparently, my life no longer interested them.

Even though I had enough work to do, the day dragged. And instead of feeling grateful for a job and a steady paycheck, I thought of Ty and the sunsets I'd never watch. Thankfully, the rain stopped when I left work, but the dark clouds remained and followed me to River City.

Instead of going to the campground, I knew I had to go to Mom's. A little before eight, I parked and walked into the house. I tilted my head at the pounding and followed the sound to the living room. "What?" I shook my head and watched Mom punctuate each of her steps with a hard rap of her cane to the floor.

She stomped closer. "Sal, I'm going stir crazy." Her fingers wove through her pink and green hair. "Want to go to The Club?"

Instead of saying I was tired, I agreed. She needed friends and to socialize. Thirty minutes later, I sat at the bar, sipping a diet soda and listening to the band.

The buzzing phone drew my attention.

Ty.

—*Are you in town?*—

—*Yes, at The Club.*—

Twenty minutes later, he leaned close. "Mind if I sit down?" He brushed a kiss across my lips and slipped onto the vacant barstool. He ordered a beer, and when his glass arrived, he raised it. "To new adventures."

I hesitated. "Just a summer adventure." I watched the smile melt from his face.

"Can I ask why?"

"No pension and barely enough savings to pay for a couple of months of storage fees."

After a long pull from his beer, he rested his thumb beneath my chin. "There will always be an excuse why you can't come, but I'm hoping you'd be brave enough to push the reasons aside and say *yes*. I'm not asking for an answer, only for you to reconsider leaving with me after the house closes."

Knowing the agony of watching the future you planned getting ripped from you like a full Brazilian wax had me wanting to say yes, but I couldn't. "I'll think about it."

An hour later, I had Mom back in bed. I told her I was going to Ty's, but I'd return to make breakfast. The sun had already set, and only a few campfires still glowed. In the distance, I could hear music and voices, but nothing distinguishable. In the trailer, I plopped down onto the loveseat.

Ty programed the music from his phone to the speakers before sitting.

The warmth from his body, the weight of his arm behind my head, the lyrics of the songs....my laughter broke through the silence as I turned and made eye contact.

"What?" He cocked his right eyebrow.

"Subtle, all these songs are about courage and change."

He pulled me closer. "You don't need songs. All you need is to look at your accomplishments this summer. You have a motorcycle license. Completed renovations on the house, gave your mom back her independence, and made this a summer worth remembering. I love you."

The quickening of my heart and a mix of overwhelming joy rushed through me. "I love you, too." The connection and bond between us deepened as I snuggled against him.

In the morning, with the sun shining through the windows, I awoke feeling invincible. His love strengthened me, and somehow, I knew saying goodbye would be easier. In the kitchen, I slid my arms around him. "I might not have gone sky diving, but I feel like this summer I really lived. Thank you for asking me to dance."

He brushed a thumb under my chin, tilting my head. "I love you, too." He lowered his mouth and kissed me.

The electric jolt of hearing those words had not diminished in the past few hours. Feeling the warmth of his embrace, I sighed and leaned back. "I'm going to Mom's."

He tried to pull me closer.

"Responsibility calls. Today, I'll help her go through the remaining stuff to determine what she wants to take and the rest she can donate."

With one last kiss, he promised he'd try to swing

by later. I stepped out of the trailer only to realize my car was at Mom's.

He stood in the doorway, grinning and dangling the keys. "Don't worry. I'll get a ride or run over later."

I smiled, certain he'd look great in shorts after a five-mile run, his skin glistening…

After climbing into the front of the cab and peering over the hood, I wondered if he had planned for me to take the truck. One more brave thing added to my list: driving and parking a dually, long box truck. At Mom's, I got lucky and found a space on the street where I didn't need to parallel park the monster.

I made Mom an omelet but only poured coffee for myself.

"What's up?" Mom pointed to my cup. "Did you already eat?"

"Not hungry."

"Instead of moping like you're thirteen, ask Ty to stay or go with him. If you don't ask—"

"I've already had the conversation."

"What?" Mom's fork rattled on her plate. "The guy's a fool for not asking you along. I can see the emotion in his eyes when he talks and how he always looks at you. He loves you."

"No." I shook my head. "He asked me to go, but I can't. There is no way I can find a remote job."

"He's buying the motorcycle."

"The money won't last long. Besides, there's too much risk. I could be on the road with him, and if there is an argument and he asks me to leave, then what?" I shrugged.

"No sense in telling you what to do. You never listen. I get that you're scared and don't like risks. I'm scared, too. What if I hate living in an apartment, or I never find love again? I know I'm going to die, but how, when, and where? Your daddy was scared, too. He didn't want to go to war and made me promise if he didn't come back, I'd love and live enough for the both of us."

"My dad was just a teenage kid, and you were, too." I swallowed at the sudden tightness in my throat.

She crossed her arms over her chest. "After I got the telegram, I wanted to climb into my bed and never get out, but then I remembered his words, *live*—" Her voice broke.

"Mom, I love you." I wrapped my arms around her and felt her tremble. "You're the bravest woman I know and did an amazing job living life."

Sputtering, she pushed back. "Hush, you sound like you're burying me."

The heaviness lifted from my shoulders. Somehow, knowing my parents weren't always brave made me feel less like a fool, but the sentiment did nothing for the sadness in my heart.

As I washed up the breakfast dishes, I read Ty's text that he and his brothers were coming over. Amber had a buyer anxious to see the house.

Instead of sorting through Mom's things, I raced around, getting everything in order. A little before three, everyone drove over to The Club, ordered sodas, and waited for news from the agent.

A little after four, Amber arrived at The Club with an offer on the house and a three-week closing date.

Mom ordered champagne.

Amber filled and passed out glasses.

"A toast to Ty getting on the road." Mom held out

her glass. "To me, getting an indoor pool and a big thanks to everyone's help."

Glasses clinked.

I took a small sip and tried to swallow. *Twenty-one days.* Ty will be gone in less than a month...three more weekends.

"Happy days!" Mom cheered. "Drink up, Sal!"

A man with long gray hair and a bushy beard walked over. "What's all the hollering about?"

I recognized him as the man I knocked over at Wake and Bakery and apologized again.

Mom gave me a slight jab to the ribs as she retold the story with quite a few embellishments.

Heat stung my cheeks, and eventually, I joined everyone in laughing.

After a few more toasts, Travis and Trevor stood.

"Come here, Sal." Travis held open his arms.

I stepped into his embrace and felt the comfort of a friend. "Thanks for helping my mom."

"You make him a better man," he whispered. "Thank you."

"I want a hug, too." Trevor pushed Travis.

Before responding, I was rocking and swaying in Trevor's bear hug.

Ty stood. "Unhand Sal."

"Come on, Amber, I'll buy you dinner." Trevor shrugged.

I exchanged a glance with Ty and watched him shrug. "Well, Mom, it looks like you're stuck having dinner with us."

"You have fun and don't worry about me. I'll get a ride home." Mom winked.

Ty captured my hand. "So, anything in particular?

Want a fancy place or laid-back?"

"Something happy. I feel melancholy. Instead of thinking about nothing being the same, I want to enjoy the evening."

On the sidewalk, he pulled me close and hugged me.

I waited for familiar phrases. Change is hard for everyone. You can do this, but instead of words, he squeezed a little tighter.

We ended up at a waterfront restaurant with a band. The place filled up fast with lots of laughter and chatter. After a delicious meal, the two of us strolled around the river park. Lost in my thoughts, I walked without talking. The only thing he could say to change the outcome would be to ask me to marry him. I wasn't a gambler and needed the security of a marriage license. Even the image of me being in the nursing home telling strangers…I could have run away with the handsome man with a fancy camper…wasn't enough to get me to go without having a ring on my finger…was I looking for excuses to hide my fear?

He steered us to a bench and sat.

I watched the distant lights of a tugboat, tucked myself into the crook of his arm, and sighed. "Part of me wants to say *yes*, but fear holds me back. I like a sure bet."

His lungs expanded beneath my head and then deflated. "Life doesn't come with guarantees. Want to go home?" He brushed a kiss across my forehead.

"To the trailer?" Suddenly, everything seemed to be on unfamiliar ground, and instead of assuming, I needed to ask.

"Is there another home?" He tugged me from the

bench.

For the remainder of the evening, I pushed aside any thoughts of goodbye.

On Sunday, I helped Mom go through a few items before heading back to the city. Of course, I promised I'd be back the following weekend. When Ty walked me to the car, our goodbye lingered.

He rocked me against his chest. "Be brave, be fearless, and be mine."

Inside the car, I took several breaths. Did I have enough courage to leave my job and go on the road? I swiped my damp palms across my thighs and drove across the bridge. The river, trees, and bluff blurred as I drove. *Maybe* kept popping into my thoughts.

The days dragged, but evenings were a blur as I put the finishing touches on his quilt. Joe and Lisa tried hard to cheer me up at lunch. On Friday, I told them about Ty's proposal to travel with him and my refusal.

"That's crazy." Joe accompanied the statement with a wild gesturing of his hands. "You can't quit work and move. Next, he'll be asking you to join a motorcycle gang."

Lisa sighed. "I've got a lot of family in the cities, but if someone asked me to go, then I'd be tempted."

"Really?" I pulled my sandwich from a bag.

She shrugged. "I know I'd at least consider it. Imagine—"

Tucking a few stray hairs behind my ears, I rolled my eyes. "I know, imagine I'm in a nursing home…" I buried my face in my hands. "For the rest of my life, I will miss Ty and the thought of walking through this door for the next eighteen years fills me with loathing, but it's too much change, too soon." I stood and tossed the remains of my lunch in the garbage. "I'll never look at another sunset again."

****

Later that evening, cuddled against Ty in the bowlegged lawn chair, I watched the flames lick at the logs.

Ty pulled his new quilt tighter around us. "I'm not so sure about having the beautiful masterpiece outside."

"Don't worry, it's washable. Promise to send me pictures of all the places the quilt travels to." I flipped the corner over and showed him how I had incorporated the heart needing a home into the blanket.

"Come with me."

Shocked he had asked me again, I hesitated as the euphoria of knowing he still wanted me increased my pulse, but I pushed the feelings aside and shook my head. "What if I quit my job and can't find another? What if I get sick or hurt? How will I pay my bills?"

He shifted, peered into my eyes, and brushed his thumb beneath my chin. "What if you give up a job you don't love, an apartment with a view that never changes, and neighbors who clomp across your ceiling? What if you stay with someone who loves you?" He nodded as his smile turned a bit crooked and way too sexy.

I kissed him, hoping he'd know I wanted to stay.

"Life, love, and living come with no guarantees. The question you need to answer is, in two weeks, will I kiss you goodbye or goodnight?"

Again, I pushed away thoughts of tomorrow and chose to enjoy every moment with him, instead.

The following two weeks flew by. I obtained the title to the motorcycle and had helped Mom pack. I sat on one of the boxes, wiping the sweat from my brow. "Excited?"

Mom shook her conservative blue spikey hair. "Yes and no. I have a lot of memories in this house, and I feel like I'm saying goodbye to Bernie all over again. But like your daddy, he's not here, and I am. So, now I need to love and enjoy life enough for both men." She smiled. "What about you? Happy about staying in the cities?"

"He hasn't even hooked up his trailer, and I already miss him."

Mom patted my hand. "Are you coming down next Thursday for the closing?"

"Ty wants to buy the motorcycle with his proceeds from the house, so I'll come down on Friday to transfer the title." I tried to swallow the lump in my throat. How could I say goodbye?

The move went smoothly, and Mom bought everyone dinner at The Club, but Ty and I couldn't wait to return to the trailer.

I didn't talk about the upcoming move. I let my body convey what I couldn't say with words.

****

When I got home on Sunday, I pulled into the apartment parking lot and slammed on my brakes when Cat Lady stepped in front of my car. I jerked forward and back as my purse flew from the seat, spilling onto the floor. I shifted into Park and jumped out of the car. "Are you okay? Did JR contact you?"

"Muffy! She snuck out, and now, I can't find her." She clutched at her chest. "What do I do?"

I collected a flashlight and helped her search. A little after midnight, I found Muffy behind a bush.

"Thank you," Cat Lady gushed as she hugged the kitten. "It wasn't like I was unhappy before I got her. But now that she's in my life, I can't imagine what I'd do without her."

I nodded. In five days, I'd be kissing Ty goodbye, and I, too, had difficulty imagining life without him. Back in my car, I gathered my belongings from the floor, holding the stone with *Believe* etched into the surface. *Believe.*

On Monday, as I dressed for work, fragments from a dream about my dad drifted through my thoughts. I couldn't recall the circumstances or the conversation, but I felt comforted. I was made of strong stuff, and being scared was just an emotional response to an unfamiliar situation.

At work, I stepped from the car, found a dime, and slid the coin into my pocket. Once again a feeling of calm settled in my stomach. *Maybe, I should…*

"Hey." Joe waved his arms as he jogged over with Lisa trailing behind.

I glanced between them as goose bumps appeared on my forearms. They were up to something. Today wasn't my birthday. "What's up?"

Lisa shrugged. "How was Ty? Did you do anything fun?"

Joe nodded. "Yeah, how was your weekend? Did you get your mom moved?"

Yawning, I half attempted to cover my mouth. "If we're continuing this conversation, I need coffee."

Lisa stepped in front of me. "That's why we are in the parking lot. We are taking you out this morning."

"Yeah, I'm driving."

I watched the subtle exchange between the two.

215

The tension in my shoulders lessened. If he had bad news, he'd be wringing his hands, pacing, and avoiding eye contact. "I'll play along until I get my coffee."

Joe parked in front of a white two-story wood house with a giant red rooster in the front yard. "Coffee Crow, they have the best cranberry scones, blueberry muffins, and the Iced Maple Latte or Salted Carmel Mocha are…" He made kissing sounds with his lips.

I followed the two through the front door of the house. I inhaled the rich smell of ground coffee beans and the sweet undertones of freshly baked bakery items.

"Go find a place to sit. I'll order." Joe brushed a hand towards me.

I glanced at Lisa and watched her shrug as she gazed around the room. The only person who looked familiar with the surroundings was Joe. "Are you sure?"

"Don't worry, I know what you gals like."

I walked down a narrow hallway, and the space opened to a sunroom. An unoccupied wooden table with mismatched chairs stood in the corner. I sat and narrowed my gaze at Lisa. "What's up? I won't tell Joe you told me."

Lisa rested her elbows on the table and leaned closer. "I don't want you to stay, and Joe's worried you're depressed with Ty and your mom moving on. I spoke to the other phone reps, and they agreed to cover for you this morning."

"Thanks. You guys are so much more than co-workers, you're friends."

"We are—so tell me. How are you doing?"

"Last night, I had the strangest dream about my dad. This morning, I found a dime. I think, maybe—"

"What are you two whispering about?" Joe set a tray of coffees and scones on the table.

"Nothing much, just you're worried she's depressed, and I think she's a fool." Lisa shrugged.

"I can hear you. What cup is mine?" I looked at the mismatched ceramic mugs with steam and froth.

Joe placed a coffee in front of me before sitting and sliding a cup to Lisa. "The scones are all cranberry, so it doesn't matter which one you pick."

The creamy milk topping with the strong brew espresso was delicious. I swiped the froth from my upper lip. "This weekend, Ty asked me again to go with him, and the thought of leaving made me nervous and anxious, but now I'm thinking maybe those feelings aren't something to run from but to embrace. I was sweating and shaking when I testified against JR, but it was the right thing to do. And now I think, maybe…"

Lisa nodded. "I agree. Wendy always told me to don't be the person crossing days off of the calendar marking time, be the person who lives every minute of each day."

By the time we left the shop, I was no longer yawning.

Joe nudged me on the way into work. "I got you a triple shot, so you should be good for the rest of the day." He winked.

After tossing my lunch into the refrigerator, I headed down the hall, turned the corner, and gasped. Heart-shaped balloons crowded my workstation, strings of hearts hung from the ceiling, and confetti littered the floor. I turned and stared at Lisa and Joe standing behind me, clapping.

Blinking back tears, I knew what I had to do.

On Friday, I arrived at the campground around seven, and even though I had put on an extra deodorant, my armpits were damp. The only thing not wet was my mouth, I felt like I had eaten a bag of cotton balls.

Ty rushed over to the car. He opened the driver's door, peered inside, and his facial features froze somewhere between a smile and surprise. "Sally, why is all this stuff in your car?"

I tried to swallow as I stretched my feet to the ground. This was going to be the best or worst moment of my life, trembling I clutched the door frame for support. "Ty."

He remained fixed.

As I looked into his unwavering blue eyes, I immediately forgot what I wanted to say. For two hours, I had rehearsed everything I'd say and all of Ty's responses; yet, looking at him I couldn't get the words to form. What if he changed his mind...made other plans? "Ty, I, um." This was more difficult than I imagined. I drew in a breath. "Can I ? Do you? Will I?"

"Sal, what is it?" He clutched my hand. "Spit it out. I'm not even sure I'm breathing?"

I closed my eyes. "Can you can find room in the trailer for my things."

He grasped my shoulders, pulled me in for a hug, then pushed me to arm's length. "Sal?"

I peered from beneath my partial closed eyelids. "Yes."

"What are you asking?"

"Ty, I want to come with you. I don't want to kiss you goodbye. I only want to always kiss you goodnight."

He gathered me against his pounding heart. "Of

course." He rained kissed over my face before dropping onto one knee. "Sal, you have made me the happiest man. Make me happier. Marry me."

"What?" I covered my mouth with my hands and bounced on the tips of my toes. "Oh, oh, oh. Are you proposing?"

He plucked a dandelion from the ground. "I don't have a ring, but I have this weed. The bright-yellow color is how I feel when I'm with you—happy, sunny, and hopeful." He stood holding the flower.

I pinched the stem between my thumb and index finger, knowing I'd treasure this moment forever. "You know with time the bright petals will turn to white fluffy fuzz. Are you absolutely sure? We don't have to be married."

"I want to call you my bride, and I'm not in love with your hair."

Melting into his kiss, I never imagined anyone could be this happy. Tears streamed down my cheeks.

He stepped back. "This was probably the worst proposal in the world, but I have to ask, Sal will you marry me?"

"Yes. A thousand times, yes." I wrapped my arms around him. "I've never heard sweeter words more eloquently spoken. You're everything I've always wanted and more."

That evening, I kissed Ty goodnight.

"Not so fast." He pulled me back into his arms. "This is the first goodnight kiss for years and years, and I want to remember this moment."

The next day, we drove to Mom's and shared the news. She smirked. "Bernie and I had this all planned. He knew Ty wanted the bike and that would be the easiest way to get you two stubborn heads to work together. Just a minute." She held out her hand and rushed into her bedroom. A moment later, she returned carrying a small black jewelry box. "He wanted you to have this, Ty."

He pulled out two gold bands.

"Your dad bought the rings, but since I never agreed to getting married, he tucked them in a drawer and—" She sniffled and swiped the back of her hand across her eyes. "Come here and give this sentimental fool a hug."

A week later, after a whirlwind wedding, Ty hooked up the fifth wheel, and the two of us drove across the bridge into Minnesota.

****

Ty's first stop was the No-Kill Dog Shelter in Minneapolis.

Pulling into the parking lot, I gasped. "Where are you going?"

"Come on, you'll see."

Inside, he walked up to the adoption counter. "I'm here to pick up Sushi."

I recognized the volunteer, who rushed around the corner and hugged Ty before wrapping her arms around me.

"Your quilt is on my bed, thanks to him." She tilted her head in Ty's direction. "And I am so glad you're the one taking home Sushi. She's one lucky dog."

I shifted my gaze between them, but before I could say a word, Scruffy dog raced towards me with tail wagging. I stooped and opened my arms to the bundle of warm fur. Pressing her against my chest, I accepted the doggy kisses to my chin. "You are just the best doggy. Such a good little boy." I felt the weight of Ty's hand on my shoulder and glanced up.

He scratched the dog's chin. "Do you want her?"

"Of course. Crazy, but I love this bundle of fur." I hugged the furry neck. "But she's a boy and JR's dog."

Ty stooped next to us. "JR wasn't being honest with you. He didn't even know the dog he was walking was a female or her name. Once I knew you were in the car, I confirmed my suspicions. Sushi did not belong to JR."

The volunteer grinned. "So, Ty made sure he outbid everyone and gifted me the quilt, and all I had to do was keep Sushi until you came by to pick her up, which was no problem. She is the sweetest little girl. The best part is that you'll be happy to know JR's community service no longer involves walking dogs. He's now our kennel cleaner."

Before the sun set, I sat at the cutest little campground on the border between Minnesota and South Dakota. After taking Sushi for a walk, Ty and I sat around a campfire, taking selfies with our shaggy girl. Later, I sent the photo to family and friends to introduce our newest family member.

Three days later, after packing up, I strolled with Ty and Sushi for one last walk and placed three quilted hearts in obscure places. "I'm glad the three of us are sharing our adventure with Wendy, Bernie, and my dad."

A word about the author...

Eighteen years ago, while living in Minneapolis, Minnesota, I published children's stories, creative non-fiction, poetry, and flash fiction, then stumbled into romance, writing several short stories and a novel with The Wild Rose Press.

Then, I took a brief hiatus that lasted thirteen years. I traveled the United States in a 40' 5th wheel camper with my husband. This journey, from the Midwest to the West Coast to the East Coast, has inspired my writing. Now, we're settled in North Carolina, living the dream in a stick and brick dwelling (apartment). But, I am back to doing what I love-spinning tales that captivate and inspire.

And I'm thrilled to share two recent novels, *Chance Meeting* and *I'd Rather Kiss You Goodnight*.

Find me on social media:
https://www.ColumbusChristine.com
https://www.facebook.com/christinecolumbus/
https://x.com/ChristineLax
https://www.instagram.com/Christine_Columbus/
https://www.linkedin.com/in/christinecolumbusnet?
https://bsky.app/profile/christinecolumbus.bsky.social

Thank you for purchasing
this publication of The Wild Rose Press, Inc.

For questions or more information
contact us at
info@thewildrosepress.com.

The Wild Rose Press, Inc.
www.thewildrosepress.com